William and Air Raid Precautions

Also published by Macmillan

Just—William
a facsimile of the first (1922) edition

The William Companion
by Mary Cadogan

Just William's World – a pictorial map
by Gillian Clements and Kenneth Waller

What's Wrong with Civilizashun
by William Brown (and Richmal Crompton)

* A hardback edition of this title is available from
Firecrest Publishing Ltd, Bath, Avon

"WELL, WHAT'RE YOU STARIN' AT?" DEMANDED
WILLIAM TRUCULENTLY.
"YOU," THEY SAID SIMULTANEOUSLY.

(See page 16)

William and
A.R.P.

RICHMAL CROMPTON

Illustrated by Thomas Henry

MACMILLAN CHILDREN'S BOOKS

First published 1939

Copyright Richmal C. Ashbee

The illustrations by Thomas Henry are reproduced
by permission of the Hamlyn Group Picture Library

First published in this edition 1987 by

MACMILLAN CHILDREN'S BOOKS
A division of Macmillan Publishers Limited
London and Basingstoke
Associated companies throughout the world

British Library Cataloguing in Publication Data
Crompton, Richmal
  William and A.R.P.
  Rn : Richmal Crompton Lamburn   I. Title
  823'.912[J]   PZ7

  ISBN 0–333–43675–X
  ISBN 0–333–43676–8 Pbk

Reprinted 1987, 1991

Phototypeset by Wyvern Typesetting Ltd, Bristol
Printed in Hong Kong

Contents

An invitation from William

Join my club and becum a nOutlaw

William Brown

You can join the Outlaws Club!
You will receive
* a special Outlaws wallet containing
your own Outlaws badge
the Club Rules
and
a letter from William giving you the secret password

To join the Club send a letter with your name and address written in block capitals telling us you want to join the Outlaws, and a postal order for 45p, to

**The Outlaws Club
Children's Marketing Department
18–21 Cavaye Place
London SW10 9PG**

You must live in the United Kingdom or the Republic of Ireland in order to join.

Chapter 1

William and A.R.P.

"Well, I don' see why we shun't have one, too," said William morosely. "Grown-ups get all the fun."

"They *say* it's not fun," said Ginger.

"Yes, they say that jus' to put us off," said William. "I bet it *is* fun all right. I bet it'd be fun if *we* had one, anyway."

"Why don't we have one?"

"I asked 'em that. I said, 'Why can't we have one?' an' they said, 'Course you can't. Don't be so silly.' Silly! S'not *us* what's silly, an' I told 'em so. I bet we could do it as well as what they do. Better, come to that. Yes, I bet that's what they're frightened of—us doin' it better than what they do."

"What do they do, anyway?" demanded Douglas.

"They have a jolly good time," said William vaguely. "Smellin' gases an' bandagin' each other an' tryin' on their gas masks. I bet they bounce out at each other in their gas masks, givin' each other frights. I've thought of lots of games you could play with gas masks, but no one'll let me try. They keep mine locked up. Lot of good it'll be in a war locked up where I can't get at it. Huh!"

There was a pause, during which the Outlaws silently contemplated the absurdity of this situation.

"I told 'em I ought to be able to wear it a bit each day

jus' for practice,'' went on William. "I told 'em I wouldn't be much use in a war 'less I did. Why, anyone'd think they *wanted* me to get killed, keepin' my gas mask where I can't get at it. It's same as murder. Just 'cause of us playin' gladiators in 'em the first day we got 'em! Well, the bit of damage it did was easy to put right. It was a jolly good thing really, 'cause it sort of showed where it was weak. They said I'd been *rough* on it. Well, if war's not s'posed to be *rough* I don't know what is. Seems cracked to me to have somethin' for a war you can't be *rough* in. I bet they're rough in 'em in those ole classes they go to."

"Well, even if they won't let us go to theirs," said Ginger, "I don't see they could stop us havin' one of our own."

"No, that's a jolly good idea," said William, brightening. "A jolly good idea. They can't stop us doin' that."

"We'll call it A.R.P. Junior Branch," suggested Ginger. "Same as what they do with Conservative Clubs an' things."

"Yes," agreed William. "A.R.P. Junior Branch. An' we'll do the same things they do an' do 'em a jolly sight better. I bet they'll be jolly grateful to us when a war comes along. I bet we'll save the country while they're messin' about tryin' to remember where they put their gas masks. If they won't let me have mine, I'll make one. I bet they're quite easy to make. Jus' a bit of ole mackintosh cut round for a face an' a sort of tin with holes to breathe through. I've got an ole mackintosh an' the tin I keep my caterpillars in'd do to breathe through. It's got holes in ready, an' I bet, if caterpillars can breathe through it, I can. Only two of 'em've died."

William and Ginger canvassed the junior inhabitants

of the village that evening, and Henry and Douglas wrote out the notice and prepared the old barn for the meeting. The preparation of the old barn was not difficult. It consisted simply of an ancient packing case for William's use as lecturer and demonstrator. The audience was expected to sit on the floor. The audience generally did sit on the floor. It grumbled, but it put up with it. The notice was the work of Ginger alone. It was executed in blacking ("borrowed" from the kitchen) on a piece of cardboard broken from the box in which his mother kept her best hat. It ran:

AIR RADE PRECORSHUN
JUNIER BRANCH
ENTRUNCE FRE.

"They'll come if it's free," said Douglas, with a tinge of bitterness in his voice. "They always come to free things."

"They'll jolly well have to come," said William sternly. "What'll they do in a war if they don't know how to do it? They've gotter learn same as grown-ups. I bet they'll feel jolly silly, the grown-ups, when this war comes along an' we do it all a jolly sight better than what they do. P'raps they won't put on such a lot of swank after *that*. I bet they *knew* we'd do it better than them, an' that's why they've been tryin' to keep us out of it. Huh!"

At the time advertised for the meeting a thin stream of children began to trickle over the fields to the old barn. There were Victor Jameson and Ronald Bell—always friends and supporters of the Outlaws—Arabella Simpkin, a red-haired, sharp-featured maiden of domineering disposition, dragging after her a small sister exactly like her, and a rag, tag, and bob-tail of juveniles. With much scuffling and shouting and criticising of the accommodation provided, they settled themselves on the floor. William's mounting upon the packing case was the signal for cheers that increased in volume as the rotten wood gave way and he disappeared

"LADIES AN' GENTL'MEN," HE SHOUTED ABOVE THE UPROAR, "WILL YOU KINDLY SHUT UP AN' LISTEN TO ME? I'M GOIN' TO TELL YOU HOW TO WIN THE WAR."

backwards. He picked himself up with a not very successful attempt at dignity, smoothed back his hair, collected the scattered sheaves of his lecture notes, scowled round upon his audience, and, putting several bits of broken wood together for a platform, took his stand on it precariously.

"Ladies an' gentl'men," he shouted above the uproar, which was still far from subsiding, "will you kindly shut up an' listen to me? I'm goin' to tell you how to win the war. Well, d'you want to win the war, or *don't*

you? . . . Arabella Simpkins, shut up makin' all that noise. . . . Victor Jameson, I tell you I'm tellin' you how to win the war. . . . You'll be sorry you've not listened when it comes an' you're all blown to bits. You've gotter listen to me, if you want to win the war. D'you want to be blown to bits by bombs an' balloons an' things jus' 'cause you wouldn't shut up an' listen to me? . . . I *didn't* start her howling. She started herself. . . . Well, I only said she'd be blown to bits if she didn't listen. I *never* said I'd blow her to bits. . . . All right, *tell* your mother. I don't care. . . . All right, *take* her home an' I'm jolly glad you're goin'. . . . Shut *up*, all of you!''

After the departure of Arabella Simpkins with her small sister—the small sister still howling, and Arabella still threatening reprisals—the uproar subsided slightly, and William, purple-faced and hoarse with shouting, turned to his typewritten papers. They were the notes of Ethel's A.R.P. classes, which he had managed to abstract from her writing desk, and he had not had time to look through them before the lecture.

"Now, listen," he said, "an' I'll tell you all about these gases an' suchlike. They're"—he studied his notes with frowning concentration—"per-sis-tent! That's what they are. Per-sis-tent. Well, that's what it says here. It *mus'* be right, mus'n't it, if it says so here? An' there's one—well, it's got a long name, I won't say it to you 'cause you cun't understand it, an' it smells like pear drops. It *says* so, I tell you. Shut up. . . . No, I've not got any pear drops. I never said I'd got any pear drops. Why don't you *listen* when I'm givin' a lecture? I wouldn't give you any if I had, either, not with you not giving me any of your liquorice all-sorts last Sat'day. You *had* got some. You were eatin' 'em. Shut *up* about pear drops. I never said a bomb was made of pear drops. I said it *smelt* of 'em. . . . Well," uncertainly, "p'raps it is. P'raps it is made of pear drops. No, it doesn't say so here. . . . Well, so are you, anyway. . . . I didn't. I said the bombs *smelt* of 'em. . . . It says so here. . . . I dunno. . . . All right, if you don't want to listen, *don't*. I don't care. . . . No, I've not gotter bomb. Shut up about pear drops. I'm sick of 'em. I'm not talking about pear drops. I'm tellin' you how to win the war. . . . Well, you gotter know what bombs smell like to win a war, haven't you? I *do* know what I'm talkin' about. . . . I never said they dropped pear drops. I said they dropped bombs. I said these bombs smelt of pear drops. . . . I *dunno* why they smell of pear drops. . . . Listen," he pleaded, hastily scanning his paper, "I'll tell you somethin' else if you'll listen. . . ."

But the meeting was breaking up in disorder. Its members had seized on the subject of pear drops and refused to be diverted from it. In any case, they wanted to do something a little more exciting than sit and listen to William holding forth from a typewritten paper. William was not altogether sorry for the curtailment of his lecture. He had caught a glimpse of several lengthy and quite unintelligible words further down on the sheet and was glad to be rescued from them.

"All right," he said. "We'll do bandagin' next. We've got some bandagin' things."

Several members of his audience, however, refused to stay.

"Said he was goin' to tell us how to win the war, an' all he could do was talk about *pear drops*," they said indignantly. "*Pear drops*. Tellin' us what *pear drops* smell like. I bet we know what *pear drops* smell like all right without *him* tellin' us. Batty. That's what he is."

They lingered only to exchange a brisk volley of

insults with the Outlaws, ending on both sides when further invention failed with "Pear drop yourself!" then took their way over the field to the village to resume the normal activities of their life.

"*Now*," said William, addressing his depleted audience, "we've gotter practise bandagin'. That's what *they* do. Then, when people get blown up by these pear—I mean bombs—you can bandage 'em up. . . . Where's the bandagin' things, Henry?"

Henry, with an air of modest pride, brought out a cardboard dress-box full of a strange assortment of ribbons, straps, bits of material, with a few genuine bandages somewhat grimy and blood-stained. Henry's mother was what is known as a "hoarder", and Henry had carefully gone through the cardboard boxes of odds and ends that she kept in the spare bedroom and taken out everything that could possibly, by any stretch of imagination, figure as a "bandage". He assuaged his conscience (for Henry was a conscientious boy) by the reflection that they had been put there in case they should ever "come in useful", and that that contingency had now arrived. The real bandages he had acquired the evening before by an act of stupendous heroism— deliberately drawing blood by means of a blunt penknife on both legs and an arm.

"Gracious, child!" his mother had said. "What on *earth* have you been doing?"

"I—sort of slipped against somethin'," said Henry vaguely.

His mother was fortunately a generous bandager, and Henry had thus acquired three bandages of enormous length that, cut into smaller portions, made a brave show.

"Now," ordered William, "one of every two's gotter

have a bandage an' bandage the other. Then do it the other way round. That's what we've gotter do now. Practise bandagin' each other up for when we get blown to pieces by these pear—these bombs. Let's start on each other's heads an' work down to each other's feet. That's the way they do it. We've gotter work very hard with this. All these bits of stuff an' ribbons an' things'll do jus' as well as real bandages. Jus' to practise on. Now we'll start on heads. Have you all got somethin' to bandage with? Well, start when I say 'go' an' see who can finish first. One . . . two . . . three . . . *Go!*"

The free fight that ensued was, perhaps, only to be expected. Each pair was scuffling for the possession of the bandage even before the signal for the bandage race was given. The bandaging of heads degenerated almost at once into the punching of heads. Bandages were used as weapons to trip up, to gag, to tie up, to flick, and generally to obstruct, harass and annoy. Old scores were wiped off, new scores were accumulated— all in a gloriously carefree spirit of give and take. The barn was full of joyously shouting, scuffling, fighting boys.

At first William tried to quell the uproar.

"*Stop* it," he shouted sternly. "Stop it an' get on bandagin'. It's a *bandagin'* class, I tell you, not a wild-beast fight. Don't you want to *learn* to bandage each other when these pear——?"

At this moment Victor Jameson lassoed him from behind with a piece of black velvet that had formed the belt of Henry's mother's last year's evening dress, and he went crashing to the ground. After that he forgot about the bandaging and joined heartily in the fight, shouting encouragement and defiance to everyone round him indiscriminately. It wasn't till the bandages were reduced to shreds that they stopped, breathless and exhilarated, and surveyed the battle-field. Bits of material were in their hair and eyes and noses and all over their clothes. They looked like the survivors of a remnant sale. . . .

"I got you in a jolly good one," panted William to Ginger.

"Yes," said Ginger, "an' I got you a jolly good one back."

"You went with a jolly fine wallop when I tripped you up," panted Victor Jameson.

"Yes, an' I'd've tied you up if the bandage hadn't broke. I'd got it right round your legs."

A small boy near the door was howling loudly and asserting that someone had pinched his bandage and stuck their finger in his eye.

"I'm goin' home," he bawled. "I'm not learnin' to win no more wars. It's nothin' but people talkin' about pear drops, an' pinchin' your bandage, an' stickin' their fingers in your eyes. . . . It's not fair. . . . I'm goin' to tell my mother."

"All right," said William. "Go home. We don't want you. That's the end of the bandagin' class, anyway."

The small boy departed still howling, followed by one or two others who had fared badly in the bandage fight.

Though still further depleted in numbers, the temperature of the A.R.P. class was now considerably raised. Its members were ready and eager for the next adventure.

"Come on," said Ginger gleefully. "What do we do next?"

William looked a little doubtful.

"Well, they practise wearin' their gas masks," he said, "but we can't do that 'cause we've not got 'em. I tried makin' one with a bit of ole mackintosh an' a tin, but the tin wouldn't stay in the hole.''

A faint anxiety clouded his spirit at the memory. It had certainly been an old mackintosh, but he wasn't really sure that it was old enough to be cut up into a gas mask. He had hung it in the hall so that the hole did not show, but his mother was certain to discover it sooner or later. She might even be discovering it at that moment. . . . But the exhilaration of the bandage fight still remained, and he decided not to waste the glorious present in anticipating trouble.

"We only want things over our faces," Ronald Bell was saying. "Anythin' over our faces'd do for gas masks."

Henry had a sudden inspiration.

"Flower pots!" he yelled excitedly. "Flower pots! We've got some big 'uns. Come on!"

Whooping, shouting, leaping, they ran across the field, down the road, to Henry's home.

"Come in at the back garden," said Henry. "They're by the greenhouse. An' this is the day the ole gard'ner doesn't come. Don't make a noise."

They entered the garden gate in single file and looked warily around them. The garden was empty. No one was in sight. By the greenhouse stood piles of large red flower pots, in which the gardener meant to pot his chrysanthemums the next morning. Henry tried one on. It completely enveloped his face.

His voice came muffled, but joyous, from behind it. "Come on. Put 'em on. They make jolly fine gas masks."

Hilariously the band put the flower pots over their heads and began to leap about in wild excitement. They did not intend to do anything beyond leaping about, but the spirit of the bandage fight still lingered with them, and they were soon charging each other with re-echoing war whoops, putting on new flower pots as the old ones were shattered. They went on till no new flower pots were left, and the place was littered with fragments of pottery. Then they stopped and looked at each other in growing dismay.

Henry glanced apprehensively towards the house.

"Gosh!" he said. "It's a good thing my mother's out, an' Cook puts on the wireless loud 'cause she's deaf. Let's get away quick."

They hurried from the scene of the crime as fast as they could.

"P'raps they'll think it was an aeroplane accident or somethin'," said Ginger hopefully.

"An' p'raps they won't," said Henry. "More like they'll start on me straight away without even givin' me a chance to explain, same as they always do."

"Tell 'em we were only havin' gas-mask drill," said William. "Tell 'em it was their fault for keepin' our gas masks locked up."

"Yes," said Henry sarcastically. "Yes, that'll do a lot of good, won't it?"

A few of the more fearful spirits at this point decided that they had had enough A.R.P. practice for one day and set off homewards (by a miracle the casualties of the flower-pot fight consisted of nothing more than a few scratches), but the Outlaws, with Ronald Bell and Victor Jameson and a few other brave spirits, felt this to be a tame ending. The exhilaration of the two fights had produced a spirit of dare-devil recklessness. They were all going to get into trouble, anyway, over Henry's flower pots, and they might as well, they felt, be killed for the proverbial sheep.

"Come on," said Ginger. "Let's do somethin' else. What else do they do?"

William considered.

"Well," he said, "there *was* somethin' else. I saw it in Robert's book. It was called a jolly long name—somethin' beginnin' with De. Detramination, or somethin'. It was takin' all your clothes off an' havin' a hose pipe turned on you."

"Come on!" they shouted with whoops of joy. "Come on!"

"Come to my house," yelled Ginger. "It's nearest. An' my mother's out, too, an' the hose pipe's right at the bottom of the garden. I bet no one sees us. . . ."

It was, however, Ginger's mother, who, returning about a quarter of an hour later, came upon the disgraceful scene—a wild medley of naked boys on the lawn, wrestling and leaping about in the full play of the garden hose, manipulated by Ginger. Their clothes, which they had flung carelessly on the grass beside them, were soaked through. . . .

*　　*　　*

That, of course, and its painful sequel, should have been the end of the A.R.P. as far as William was concerned. He fully intended that it should be. He meant to have no more dealings with it of any kind. He even abandoned a secretly cherished project of turning the spare bedroom into a gas-proof chamber, as a pleasant surprise for his family ("Jolly well serve 'em right now not to have one," he said bitterly to himself). He glared ferociously at a heading in his father's newspaper, "A.R.P. Muddle", thinking at first that it must be making fun of his short-lived, but eventful, leadership of the A.R.P. Junior Branch. ("Muddle!" he muttered. "We didn't do a *thing* that wasn't in the book. *They* can go on doin' it for weeks an' weeks an' no one stops 'em, but the minute we *start* they set on us. Well, they'll jolly well be sorry when the war comes, that's all, an' it'll be their own faults.")

If it hadn't been for the local "black-out", William would not have given the thing another thought except as a faint memory of a glorious day followed by much ill-merited suffering. But the local "black-out" thrilled and impressed him, and made him long again to take his part in the great national movement. The dark roads, the shuttered windows, the blazing search-lights, the sound of the aeroplanes roaring overhead, stirred his blood, and he wanted to be up and doing—shooting down aeroplanes, or fighting with them in the search-lit sky. He took his air-gun and pointed it upwards between the drawn curtains.

"Bang, bang! That's got 'em," he muttered with satisfaction. "That's got 'em all right! Listen to 'em comin' down. That's got another. *An'* another."

As he dressed the next morning he decided that the failure of his previous attempts at A.R.P. work lay in the large number of its participants.

"When there's a lot of 'em they always start gettin' rough," he said sternly, scowling at his reflection in the mirror and brushing his hair with almost vindictive energy. "Always start gettin' rough when there's a lot of 'em. I bet if I'd done somethin' alone it'd've been all right. . . . I *bet* it would. . . ."

After breakfast he happened to see the *National Service Handbook* lying on his mother's writing desk. It had only arrived a few days before, and he had not had an opportunity of examining it yet. He took it up and turned over the pages with interest. Police. . . . Fire

Service. . . . First Aid. . . . Not much he could do. . . .
Then he began to read with interest the section headed:
"Evacuation of Children from Dangerous Areas."
"Removing children from the dangers of air attack on
crowded cities to districts of greater safety." Well, he
could help with that, all right. Anyone could help with
that. An' he'd do it himself, too, not get in a lot of other
people. It was that that had messed things up
before. . . . Hadley would come under the heading of a
crowded city, surely. . . . It had shops and streets and
rows of houses, and it was jolly crowded, especially on
market day. And—William threw a glance out of the
window—this must be a district of greater safety, all
fields and hedges and that sort of thing. Well—he could
easily fetch children in here from Hadley. He wouldn't
mind doing that. In fact, his spirits rose as he saw himself
bringing in a swarm of Hadley children, rather in the
manner of the Pied Piper of Hamelin, and establishing
them in his home, and those of his friends. He couldn't
do it till there was a war, of course, but he'd do it then,
all right. He'd start off as soon as the war broke out.
People'd be jolly grateful to him. . . .

That afternoon, having nothing much else to do, he
set out for Hadley in order to study it in its new light of
danger zone. Yes, there were quite a lot of people in the
High Street and in the Market Square. It certainly came
under the heading of "crowded city". He'd collect as
many of the children as he could as soon as the war broke
out, and escort them at once to the safer surroundings of
his home. No one could object to his doing something
that he was told to do in a book sent out by the
Government. . . .

Dismissing the subject for a time, he gave his whole
attention to examining the windows of Hadley's leading

toyshop. He spent several minutes in comparing the different merits of a 6*d*. pistol and a 6*d*. trumpet—a purely academic process, as he possessed no money at all. Having, after deep thought, decided in favour of the pistol, he was just about to move on to the sweet-shop next door in order to make a theoretical choice between the wares in that window, too, when he banged into two children who were standing watching him. They were stolid, four-square children and exactly alike—with red hair and placid, amiable expressions.

"Well, what're you starin' at?" demanded William truculently.

"You," they said simultaneously.

"Anythin' funny about me?" he said threateningly.

"Yes," they said.

This took the wind out of his sails, and he said rather flatly:

"Well, you're jolly funny yourselves, come to that. What've you done to your hair?"

"What've you done to yours?"

"Funny colour for hair, yours."

"Well, yours is all stickin' up."

"You look like a couple of Guy Fawkes."

"So do you. You look like two couples."

Friendly relations having been thus established, William continued:

"How old are you?"

"Seven."

"Both of you?"

"Yes, we're twins. How old are you?"

"Eleven. What's your names?"

"Hector an' Herbert. What's yours?"

"William. Where d'you live?"

"There. In that street."

William's gaze followed the direction of the pointing fingers. It was one of the narrow, crowded streets that ran off from the High Street—one of the streets, without doubt, from which William would have to rescue his child protégés when the time of emergency should come. It occurred to him that he might as well explain matters to the twins. There wouldn't be much time for explanation when war had actually broken out. He assumed his sternest expression and most authoritative manner.

"You've gotter be 'vacuated when war comes," he said.

"We've been it," said Herbert. "Our arms swelled up somethink awful."

"I don't mean that sort of 'vacuation," said William. "I mean, took out. Took out of crowded cities to districts of greater safety, same as it says in the book. 'Cause of bombs an' things."

Light dawned upon the twins. Their eyes gleamed. They leapt excitedly up and down on the pavement with squeals of joy. They had had staying with them recently some cousins from London who had been evacuated in the last crisis and who had told them thrilling tales of camp life—games, entertainment, unlimited food of unusual kinds, and a glorious crumbling of the whole fabric of discipline.

"Coo! Lovely!" said Hector.

Herbert looked expectantly at William and said simply:

"Come on. Let's start now."

William was somewhat taken aback by their matter-of-fact acceptance of the position. He had expected to have to explain, persuade, cajole. . . .

"Well . . ." he began uncertainly, but Herbert had already taken his hand.

"Come on," he said urgently. "Let's start off. Shall we have sausage an' fried potato for breakfast, same as they had?"

"Well . . ." began William again, and then thought suddenly that he might as well take them up to the village. It would show them the way. They would be able to help him bring the other children when the war broke out. It would save time then to have two, at any rate, who knew just where to go.

"All right," he ended. "We might as well jus' go there. . . ."

They accompanied him joyously up the hill to the village, telling him excitedly all the stories that their cousins had told them.

"They had a tug-of-war."

"They had sports every afternoon."

"They had picnics."

"They had treacle tart."

"They jus' had a few lessons, but not real 'uns."

"It was jus' like Christmas."

"They made as much noise as they liked, an' no one stopped them."

They chattered so much that William could hardly get a word in till they reached the gate of his house.

There he stopped and said a little lamely:

"Well, this is it. You'll know where to come now, won't you?"

"But we've come," said Hector simply. "We're here, aren't we?" He opened the gate. "Come on."

William hesitated, then suddenly remembered that his mother was out, that it was Cook's afternoon off and that the housemaid had been summoned to attend a sick aunt. "You'll be out all afternoon, won't you, William?" his mother had said. "I'll be home in time to get the tea, but it's no good your coming back before then, because there'll be no one in."

The Browns' house contained a cellar, which was used for the purpose of storing such things as coal, potatoes and Mrs. Brown's pickled eggs. William had heard his family discussing the possibility of using this as an air-raid shelter, and had already decided to house his evacuated children in it during air raids. It wouldn't do any harm to show it to the twins. It seemed silly to bring them all this way and then not show them their air-raid shelter. . . .

Though the front door was shut, a spare key was always kept under the edge of the mat in the porch for the use of such members of the family as happened to have forgotten their own. It wouldn't take a minute just to unlock the door and show the twins their air-raid shelter. It couldn't possibly do any harm. No one could object to that. In any case, no one need know. . . .

"I'll jus' show you the place," he said.

He took the key from under the mat, unlocked the door, and led the twins into the hall.

"What time's tea?" said Herbert, wiping his feet on the mat.

"We're going to have some games first, aren't we?" said Hector anxiously.

"Well . . ." said William, beginning to feel somewhat overwhelmed by his responsibilities. "I bet I can find you somethin' to eat, an' p'raps we can have a game of some sort. . . . Anyway, I've gotter show you the way to the cellar first. It's down here."

He opened a door under the stairs, revealing a flight of stone steps.

"Coo!" said Herbert, with obvious approval. "That's jolly fine!"

He was a boy of an adventurous turn of mind, and found this, to him, novel subterranean world preferable even to the open-air camp-life described by his cousins.

"I bet I find some hidden treasure," he added.

"Bags me find some, too," said Hector.

They went down the steps to the cellar. The light which came from a small window, lit by a grating above, was dim and ghostlike. There was a heap of coal in one corner, a sack of potatoes in another, and a sack of carrots in another. (Mr. Brown had lately read an article on the nutritive value of carrots and had bought a sack from a friend at Covent Garden.) In another stood two pails containing Mrs. Brown's pickled eggs. A broken step-ladder, a bottomless bucket, and a broken clothes-basket completed the furniture.

"You see, you'll be here while there's an air-raid goin' on," explained William.

The twins continued to survey their surroundings with approval.

"It looks a jolly int'restin' place," said Herbert. "Where do we sleep?"

"Well—upstairs, I suppose," said William, who hadn't considered that question yet.

"We'd better go back for our night things now, hadn't we?" said Hector. "We didn't bring anythin' with us."

It dawned on William for the first time that the twins considered themselves permanently evacuated, that they were contemplating forming part of the Brown *ménage* for an indefinite period. Just as he opened his mouth to correct this misapprehension, the front-door bell sounded through the house. He froze and waited in silence. It sounded again. Quickly he considered the situation. If he didn't answer it, it would probably continue to ring for some time. Moreover, the visitor, whoever it was, might, if left there too long, notice through the grating mysterious signs of life in the cellar below. Better perhaps go and answer the door, and say that his mother was not at home. Then the visitor would go away and he would be left in peace to deal with his evacuated twins.

"Wait a minute," he whispered, and went quickly up the short flight of stairs to the hall. There he carefully closed the door leading to the cellar and opened the front door. His expression was stern and forbidding.

"My mother——" he began with a fierce scowl, and stopped.

Miss Milton stood on the doorstep, holding a small paper bag in her hand.

"Oh, good afternoon, William," she said.

"'Afternoon," responded William, scowling yet more ferociously. "My mother's out. Everyone's out but me."

"Oh, that's all right, dear," said Miss Milton. "I've just brought something for her Pound Day. She asked us to send them round in the morning, I know, but I've not had a second till now."

William remembered vaguely that streams of groceries had been arriving all morning for the Pound Day of a Girls' Hostel in Hadley, for which Mrs. Brown collected local subscriptions. William hadn't been interested then, and he wasn't interested now. He held out his hand for the parcel.

"A' right," he said shortly. "I'll give it her."

"I'd like to write her a note about it, if I may," said Miss Milton, stepping past William's solidly obstructive form into the hall, and making her way to the drawing-room. William followed, his expression one vast silent protest.

She sat down at the writing table, took a piece of Mrs. Brown's writing paper, and began the note.

"You see, dear," she explained to William, as she wrote, "I've brought rice because I thought that probably no one else would think of it, but I wanted to tell her that if she'd rather have the unpolished kind—they say it's more nourishing, unpolished, you know, though I could never fancy it myself, it looks so dirty—but if she'd rather have the unpolished kind the grocer will change it. . . ."

"I'll tell her that," said William gruffly. "You needn't write it all down."

His ears were strained anxiously for suspicious sounds from below. Miss Milton was a notorious busybody. She never left anything alone till she'd got to the bottom of it.

"That's very kind of you, dear," said Miss Milton serenely, as she continued her note, "but you know, verbal messages are so apt to get distorted. I think it's so much better to have things in black and white." She murmured her words aloud as she wrote. "They'll—change—it—for—unpolished—if—you——" Then she stopped suddenly and sat listening, her whole body tense. The worst had happened. Hector and Herbert were exploring the cellar just underneath her with shouts of rapture. Their actual words could not be heard, but William could tell that they were acclaiming their discoveries to each other in careless glee.

Miss Milton put down her pen and looked at William.

"I thought, dear," she said in a low voice, still listening intently to the mysterious sounds, "that you were alone in the house."

"Yes, I am," said William.

"Then what's that?" said Miss Milton.

"What?" said William, deciding to brazen it out.

"Those voices."

"What voices?" said William, exchanging his forbidding scowl for an expression of exaggerated bewilderment.

"Can't you—hear?" said Miss Milton, dropping her voice still further.

"Hear what?" said William, whose expression now suggested that of an amiable half-wit.

"Voices," said Miss Milton again, looking about the room. "They seem to come from all around me."

William realised with something of relief that Miss Milton's sense of hearing was not very clear, and that she was not aware that the Brown house contained a cellar.

"It's prob'ly an echo," he said hopefully.

"Echo?" said Miss Milton, a little tartly. "My dear boy, an echo of *what*?"

"Well, anythin'," said William. "Echoes come from anywhere, you know. It might be jus' people talkin' miles off, an' it—well, it's just sort of echoes."

"That's nonsense, my dear boy," said Miss Milton, so firmly that William decided to abandon the echo theory.

"It's prob'ly rats, then," he tried next. "Rats or the wind. I've often noticed rats an' wind sound jus' like people talkin'."

"But *you* hear nothing," said Miss Milton. "You just said that you heard nothing."

"No, I can't hear anythin'," said William. " 'Cept— well, 'cept jus' a bit of rats an' wind."

Miss Milton listened again, still more intently, while the voices of Hector and Herbert rose muffled but vociferous from below. William cleared his throat, then coughed loud and long, but not quite loud or long enough to drown the twins' exultant yells. Then he looked at Miss Milton in surprise. Her air of bewilderment had changed to one of happy ecstasy that sat oddly upon her plain, matter-of-fact, pince-nezed face.

"Tell me, dear," she said. "Do other people hear these sounds?"

"Well, yes," said William, anxious to take her mind off the subject as quickly as possible. "Some people do. Some people hear them all right. It's jus' somethin' wrong with their ears," he went on in sudden inspiration. "That's what it is. People with somethin' wrong with their ears hear 'em. It's nothin' axshully serious, of course," he added hastily. "They jus' hear voices like that when there's somethin' wrong with their ears, that's all."

But the expression of ecstasy did not fade from Miss Milton's face.

"Oh, no, it's not that, dear boy," she said, in a dreamy, far-away voice. "It's not that. My mother was the seventh child of a seventh child, and, though this is the first manifestation I've actually experienced, I've always known that it must be there somewhere." She looked about her with a blandly complacent smile, as the voices of Hector and Herbert arose again—now in sudden altercation. "Voices everywhere. . . . All around me. . . ." She patted William's head. "Be thankful that you do not hear them, dear boy. A gift like that is a great responsibility. . . . Well," she drew herself up and spoke in a quick, brisk voice, "one still has to live in the material world of everyday life, has one not? One must not forget that. One must not allow any manifestation of another world to cause one to forget one's duty in this one, and my next duty is to go to see Mrs. Bott about mending the surplices. She always seems to be away from home her week, and I've decided to nail her down. Be sure your mother gets my note,

won't you? Well . . ." She drifted into the hall and
paused as a loud shout from Hector floated up from the
cellar. "They seem to follow me," she said, with a
seraphic smile, "to move with me as I move. . . . Well,"
resuming her brisk voice "as I said, one must not neglect
one's duty. . . ."

To William's relief she had now reached the front
door. He watched her drift down the drive, turn round
anxiously when she reached the gate, then reassured by
a yell from the twins, pass happily on her way.

"Corks!" gasped William, when she was safely out of
sight. "Corks! I thought she was never goin'. I'll get 'em
out quick 'fore anyone else comes."

He hastened down the cellar steps to find a hilarious
potato fight going on. A large King Edward hurled by
Hector at Herbert hit him on the nose as he reached the
bottom of the stairs. He firmly resisted the temptation to
join in the fight.

"We're havin' a jolly good time," panted Herbert.
"It's a jolly fine place. I wish we'd got a place like this in
our house. We're pretendin' we're smugglers an' pirates
in a cave. We're having a jolly good fight."

"Listen," said William urgently. "You've gotter go
home now. This was only a sort of practice. You——"

At that moment the front-door bell rang again.

"Corks!" groaned William. "S'like a bad dream."

Once more he weighed the advantages of answering
and not answering the bell, and once more decided in
favour of answering. But he must secure the twins'
silence. Another visitor might not be ready to ascribe
their raucous young voices to psychic origins.

"Look here," he said hoarsely. "I've gotter go for a
minute. You've not gotter make a noise. Will you
promise to be quiet while I'm away?"

"Is it the enemy?" said Hector, with eager interest.

"We've been sayin' p'raps the enemy'd come. When will they start droppin' bombs?"

Herbert threw a potato at the small, grimy window, breaking one of the panes, and shrieked excitedly:

"The enemy! The enemy! The enemy! Bomb! Bomb!"

"Shut up," said William fiercely. "It *is* the enemy, an' they *will* drop bombs if you start makin' a noise. If you're quiet they'll go away. P'raps they're goin' away now." He listened hopefully, but the only sound that broke the silence was another and more imperious peal of the front-door bell. He sighed. "No, they're not goin' away. Well, it'll be all right s'long as you're quiet, but if you start kickin' up a row they'll start droppin' bombs."

"What'll we do if they come down here?" said Hector.

"Pelt 'em with potatoes," shouted Herbert gleefully.

"Shut *up*!" said William.

Another peal of the front-door bell told him that the visitor was of the sort that never owns defeat, so, with another stern admonition to the twins not to speak till he returned, he hastened again up the cellar steps to the front door. Mrs. Monks, the vicar's wife, stood there with a small grocer's paper bag in her hand. The scowl with which William greeted her was more repellent than ever.

" 'Fraid my mother's out," he muttered gruffly.

Mrs. Monks pushed him on to one side and sailed placidly into the hall.

"I want to leave this for the Pound Day," she said, "and write her an apology for not having left it this morning, as she asked us to."

"You needn't stay'n write her a note," said William with a note almost of pleading in his voice. At present there was silence below, but at any moment, he felt, pandemonium might break out again. "I'll tell her. I'll 'splain. You can go right away now. I'll 'splain all right."

"My dear William," said Mrs. Monks, "I never believe in leaving explanations to a third party. In any case, I owe her an apology, and I must make it as nearly in person as possible. I certainly can't send it verbally, even by you. Indeed, I know how often children of your age either forget to give messages, or give them in a completely garbled form."

She laid down her paper bag and handbag on the hall chest side by side, and sailed into the drawing-room taking her place at Mrs. Brown's writing table.

"I didn't *forget* to bring my pound of rice this morning," she went on, "but my housemaid was taken ill, and I haven't had a moment till now. Not a *moment*. I got rice, by the way, because I thought that probably no one else would think of it." Her pen moved rapidly over the paper as she spoke. William stood by her, tense and rigid, listening with every nerve for sounds from below. But all was still and silent. Evidently Hector and Herbert had taken his words to heart. Once he thought he heard someone moving in the hall, but the sound ceased almost at once, and it was plain that Mrs. Monks heard nothing.

"There!" she said, signing her name with a flourish. "See she gets that, won't you? Well, I must hurry off now." She collected her handbag from the hall chest and sailed to the front door. "Be *sure* you give her my note. . . . *Good*-bye."

William heaved a sigh of relief as she sailed down the drive and disappeared into the road. The danger was over. He could now dispose of the twins before his mother came back, and—His heart sank again. Another

figure was coming up the drive, carrying a grocer's paper
bag. Too late even to pretend that there was no one in
the house, as he had decided to in case of future
interruptions, for she had seen him and was waving to
him gaily. It was Miss Thompson, who lived with her
aunt at The Larches. She was small and fluttery, like a
bird, and she wore a hat with a perky little feather
sticking up in front like a bird's top-knot.

"Is your mother in?" she said breathlessly, as she
reached the front door. "Aren't I *naughty*? I quite
forgot about bringing my pound this morning. I've no
excuse at all. I just forgot! I bought a new hat in Hadley
this morning, and I'm afraid it drove everything else out
of my mind." She fluttered into the hall and looked at
herself in the mirror. "It's rather nice, isn't it?" she said.
"I thought it was a bit too young at first, but the woman
persisted that it wasn't. She said everyone was wearing
them, and that it was *quite* suitable. It's just a *leetle* on
the small side. It gave me a headache even in the shop,
and it's coming on again now. I must take it back to be
stretched. I'll just slip it off now while I write my note of
apology to your mother. It will give my head a rest."

"I'll tell her," said William desperately. "You
needn't write. You can go home an' rest your head
prop'ly. . . ."

But she wasn't listening to him. She was putting her
hat and grocer's bag on the hall chest, side by side, and
chattering away in her birdlike inconsequential fashion.

"I see I'm not the only naughty one. I do hope your
mother will forgive me. Such a little scatter-brain, I
always am! I got rice. I thought that probably no one else
would think of it. And it's so wholesome. Whole tribes
live on it in India. Now may I just go into the drawing-
room, and write my little note? I *do* hope she won't be

cross with me. I thought of it first thing this morning and then, as I said, the hat drove it clean out of my mind. May I sit here and use a piece of her notepaper? 'Dear— Mrs.—Brown. . . .' "

William watched her helplessly, his body rigid, his ears strained. Once he thought again that he heard stealthy sounds outside the room, but decided it must be his imagination.

" 'Please—forgive——' " said Miss Thompson, slowly ending her note, " 'your—scatter-brained— friend—Louisa—Thompson.' There!" She fastened up the envelope. "Now I must fly. *Literally* fly. My aunt wanted to have tea early to-day and——" She glanced at the clock. "My *goodness*! I'm late already. I shouldn't have come till after tea. What a *scatter-brain* I am! Forgive me, dear. I can't stop to hear all your news, though I'd love to." She fluttered into the hall, snatched up her hat without looking at it, perched it on her head, said, "Good-bye, good-bye, good-bye! Give my love to your dear mother," and fluttered off down the drive.

William closed the door and drew a long, deep breath.

"Crumbs!" he said, in a tone of heartfelt relief.

The next step was plain. Now that the coast was clear all he had to do was to bring the twins from their hiding-place and speed them on their homeward way. But, before he'd had time even to reach the cellar door, there was the sound of a key in the lock, and his mother entered.

"Hello, dear!" she said. "I never thought you'd get back before me. I came back earlier than I intended, anyway. . . . Oh, dear! Rice again. No one seems to be able to think of anything else but rice. Still, the grocer says he'll change it. . . . Now there's only you and me, dear, so we'll have a nice cosy tea together. And you'll help me get it ready, won't you? You can be such a help when you like."

Despairingly, he watched Mrs. Brown hang her hat and coat on the hatstand, then read the three notes that were on the hall chest with the three bags of rice. He could hear faint sounds from the cellar below. They began to increase in volume.

"Mother," he said, speaking in a loud, booming voice, in order to drown them, "wouldn't you like to go an' lie down for a bit while I get tea? Jus' about five minutes." (He could easily get rid of the twins in five minutes.) "You—you look a bit tired to me. You look 's if it'd do you good to have a bit of a lie-down while I get tea."

Mrs. Brown gazed at him tenderly, deeply touched by this proof of his affection and considerateness, storing up the incident in her mind in order to tell her husband when he came home from work. ("I'm always telling you that you don't do William justice, dear. Now just listen to what he said to me when I came in this afternoon. . . .")

"That's a very kind thought, dear," she said, "but I'm not feeling at all tired, and I certainly won't let you get the tea all alone. Many hands make light work, you know. Now I'll put the kettle on, and you get out the tablecloth and——"

"Mother," said William with the urgency of desperation (again his ears, strained to attention, had caught those faint sounds from below), "it seemed to me someone'd stole a lot of tools from our tool shed this afternoon. Seemed to me quite a lot of them'd gone when I came in." (If only he could get her out of the house as long as it would take to go to the tool shed and back, it would give him time to drag the twins up from their retreat and hustle them off home.)

"What had gone, dear?" Mrs. Brown said placidly.

"Well," temporised William, "I can't say *quite* what'd gone. I didn't count 'xactly. I only saw that *some'd* gone. I thought I'd better tell you. . . ."

"I expect you're mistaken, dear," said Mrs. Brown, bustling about the kitchen, quite unmoved by the news. "You're always imagining things. I'll look after tea, but I'm certainly going to have a cup of tea before I do anything else. Anyway, if they're gone, they're gone, and a few minutes won't matter here or there. . . . Have you got the cloth out, dear?"

"Mother . . ." said William. (He was going to tell her that he thought he'd heard the boiler burst just before she came in. That should get her up to the loft at any rate.) But at that moment there came another ring at the front-door bell.

"See who it is, dear," called his mother.

William went to the door. Miss Milton entered. There was a tense, keyed-up look on her face.

"I'm so sorry," she said in a tense, keyed-up voice to Mrs. Brown, who had come out of the kitchen to see who it was. "I'm terribly sorry, but I *must* make sure."

"Make sure?" said Mrs. Brown.

"Yes," said Miss Milton. "It was here I heard them. They seemed to follow me to the gate, then stopped. I've not heard them since. I *had* to come back here and—make sure. Can I still hear them here? I know I did before. Often that—extra sense, shall we call it?—functions erratically, but one must do what one can to understand it, to regularise it. . . . I felt that I *must* make sure whether I could still hear them here. . . ."

"Them?" faltered Mrs. Brown.

She'd always known that Miss Milton was a little

eccentric, but—well, really, eccentric was almost too mild a word for this.

"The voices," said Miss Milton.

"The voices?"

"Yes."

Miss Milton had stridden into the drawing-room, and was standing there in the middle of the room, every muscle taut as if poised for flight.

"I heard them here," she said dreamily, "only a few minutes ago. Voices. All round me."

She listened, but there was no sound. The twins had evidently discovered some silent occupation for the moment. Mrs. Brown was too much bewildered for speech, and William realised the uselessness of it.

"Strange!" said Miss Milton. "Either the gift has deserted me or——"

At that moment came another interruption. It was Mrs. Monks. Admitted by William, she sailed into the drawing-room, her face set and stern, and, opening the small handbag she carried, drew out three or four carrots.

"What's the meaning of this?" she said severely.

Mrs. Brown sat down upon the nearest chair.

"What on earth is happening?" she said helplessly.

"I came here a few minutes ago," said Mrs. Monks, "to leave my rice and write a note of apology——"

"Fancy you thinking of rice!" put in Miss Milton, who had now decided that the gift had deserted her.

"I laid my handbag on the hall chest while I came in to write my note," continued Mrs. Monks, ignoring Miss Milton. "I had met the organist just before I reached your gate and had opened my bag to consult my diary because we were discussing the most suitable day for the choir treat. The bag then held its usual contents—my purse, stamp book, engagement diary and—er—a small powder compact. As I said, I laid it down on your hall chest for a matter of—say—five minutes and when I got home I found that it contained—*these*!" She held out the carrots dramatically.

Mrs. Brown looked at William. William looked at the carrots and understood now only too well those faint sounds he had heard in the hall while Mrs. Monks was writing her note. . . .

"William!" said Mrs. Brown reproachfully.

With obvious reluctance, Mrs. Monks exonerated William.

"Well, it couldn't have been William," she said. "Not *actually* William, at least. William was in here with me all the time."

"But who could have done it, then?" said Mrs. Brown. "William, you didn't bring any of your friends home with you, did you?"

"No, Mother," said William, assuring himself that neither Hector nor Herbert came under the category. "No, Mother, I didn't bring any of my friends home."

"But I can't *think*——" began Mrs. Brown, when Miss Thompson entered. She entered in her usual bird-like, fluttering manner, but she suggested now a bird in deep distress. She wore perched on her head a little plain, untrimmed hat.

"I found the front door open, and so I just came in," she said. "Mrs. Brown, I don't know *what* to do. I can't think *what's* happened. . . ."

"Happened?" said Mrs. Brown, in a faint voice.

"To my hat," said Miss Thompson. "I only bought it this morning. I *came* in it when I came to bring my rice." ("Rice!" put in Mrs. Monk, and Miss Milton in indignant surprise.) "It had a band of ribbon round it

THE ROOM SPUN ROUND MRS. BROWN. SHE CAUGHT HOLD
OF THE TABLE NEXT HER TO KEEP IT STILL.

and a little feather in the front. William knows it had. He
saw it. I showed it him. I looked at it in the glass. I took it
off because it was making my head ache, and put it on
the chest while I came in here to write my note, and then
I put it on again—Oh, very carelessly and without
looking because I'm such a scatter-brain, you know—

but when I got home and took it off I found that the trimming had gone.

The room spun round Mrs. Brown. She caught hold of the table next to her to keep it still.

WILLIAM'S FACE WORE A FIXED AND GLASSY LOOK OF
HORROR.

William's face wore a fixed and glassy look of horror. Gosh! They'd been up both times. They'd taken the things out of Mrs. Monks's handbag and the trimming from Miss Thompson's hat.

"The trimming gone?" repeated Mrs. Brown feebly.

"Yes," said Miss Thompson. "The trimming gone. It was quite untrimmed when I got home. It couldn't have *fallen* off. A band of ribbon and a feather can't *fall* off a hat while it's on the head. I know I'm a scatter-brain, but I'm quite sure of that. It must have been taken off, and it must have been taken off here while I was writing my note. . . . And it couldn't have been William, because he was with me all the time."

Mrs. Brown raised a hand to her head. She looked from the carrots that Mrs. Monks was still holding out accusingly, to the plain, straw hat in Miss Thompson's small, clawlike hand.

"I—I don't understand," she said. "I mean—who *could* it have been?"

"A poltergeist" said Miss Milton, in a tone of deep satisfaction. "I've read about them in psychic papers. That was what I heard, and that was what put carrots in Mrs. Monks's bag and took the trimming off Miss Thompson's hat."

"Stuff and nonsense!" said Mrs. Monks rudely. "Anyway, what I want to know is, where my purse and engagement diary have got to, and where Miss Thompson's feather is? *That's* the question."

Mrs. Brown made a supreme effort to recover her faculties.

"William," she said, "do you know anything at all about this?"

William was saved from answering by a loud noise from below. It sounded like—and probably was— someone sliding down a heap of coal.

They stared at each other in silence for a few seconds, then Mrs. Brown went from the room to the cellar door and stood there listening. The others followed slowly.

"There's someone in the cellar," she said at last, her face paling as she turned to them. "I can hear them moving about quite plainly."

A thief in the cellar was something definite, something one could, to a certain extent at any rate, deal with, and Mrs. Brown's usual matter-of-fact manner returned to her. With a quick movement she twisted the key in the lock, then turned to William.

"William, go round to the police station at once and fetch Sergeant Perkins. It's no use ringing them up," she went on to the others, "because, if you do, the stupid one always answers and he's deaf as well. Run as fast as you can William. Tell Sergeant Perkins that I've got a man—say a *dangerous* man—locked in the cellar, and that he'd better bring help in case he's violent. I was saying only the other day that that cellar's not safe. A thief could so easily remove the grating and force the window and then conceal himself there till everyone was in bed. Hurry up, William! Don't stand dawdling there. Run all the way. . . ."

William went out of the front door, his face set like the face of a sleepwalker. Long ago he had given up all hope of being able to control the situation. He was now the blind tool of Fate. . . .

The three women stood by the cellar door, watching the keyhole anxiously, as though it might unlock itself if not kept under close observation.

"You did *lock* it, didn't you?" said Miss Milton apprehensively. "It would be rather a catastrophe if it *had* been locked and you'd unlocked it."

"No," said Mrs. Brown. "It's all right." She tried the key again. "It's quite safe."

"I wonder if he knows we know," said Mrs. Monks. "I hope he isn't *planning* anything." Then a sudden thought struck her and she said: "But, Mrs. Brown, that doesn't explain the carrots."

"Nor my feather," said Miss Thompson.

Then suddenly there came from the cellar another sound of falling coal, followed by a peal of unmistakably childish laughter.

"It's—children," gasped Mrs. Brown.

"So it is," said Mrs. Monks. Her nervousness vanished abruptly. Children. She knew how to deal with children. She could control a whole Sunday-school by the flicker of an eyelash. There was no choirboy in existence so unquellable that she could not quell him at once. . . . She seemed to grow several inches taller as she assumed her official manner.

"Let me deal with this," she said. "To begin with, at any rate. I'll go down first, alone. If I need help I'll call. . . ."

"But, Mrs. Monks——" began Mrs. Brown anxiously.

Mrs. Monks paid no attention to her. With the air of a general at the head of a large army she marched down the cellar steps. At the bottom the dim light from the grating showed her the whole scene in a moment— Herbert as a Red Indian, wearing round his head the trimming of Miss Thompson's hat, Hector as the Pale Face (his face paled by Mrs. Monks's powder compact), and, ranged in a small box, the contents of Mrs. Monks's handbag, by means of which the Pale Face had been purchasing native food (such as carrots and potatoes). Many half-eaten carrots lay about them on the floor. Their persons revealed generous traces of the coal-heap, which they had utilised for "shooting the rapids". But this scene lasted only a moment. William had warned the twins that the enemy might come, and the twins had prepared a heap of ammunition in readiness for the contingency. No sooner had Mrs. Monks taken in this amazing scene than one of Mrs. Brown's pickled eggs caught her full on the forehead, and another on her mouth, which she was opening for a majestic reproof. Almost immediately afterwards a large piece of coal struck her on the chest. Mrs. Monks was a brave woman. She had once shoo'ed out a dangerous bull that had strayed into the Vicarage garden, and it had obeyed her meekly. But she was winded, choked and blinded. Dripping with coal and egg, she staggered up the cellar steps to rejoin the other three. They stared at her in blank dismay.

"There are two children down there," she said indistinctly, but with as much dignity as could possibly be mustered in the circumstances. "Two children. Quite small, but—I think I'll sit down for a moment. I seem to have swallowed an egg shell. . . ."

From below came the voices of the twins, now unrestrained and exultant.

"We're bombing the enemy," they shouted. "We're bombing the enemy! The enemy! The enemy! We're bombing the enemy!"

"Come along, Miss Thompson," said Mrs. Brown firmly. "We must do something at once."

They descended the steps—only to return a few moments later in much the same condition as Mrs. Monks.

"There's no getting near them," gasped Mrs. Brown, wiping egg out of her eye.

"The little villains!" panted Miss Thompson. "My poor feather! Oh, dear, I've swallowed such a big piece of coal. I hope it won't do me any harm."

"Of course it won't," said Mrs. Monks curtly.

"Carbon's good for the digestion."

From below the exultant shouts increased in volume to the accompaniment of breaking eggs. Herbert and Hector were evidently carrying on a glorious fight.

"Bombing the enemy!" and they continued to shout: "Bomb! Bomb! Bomb! Bomb! Bomb!"

"My poor eggs!" moaned Mrs. Brown. "I put down eight dozen."

Then William returned. He had no suspicion of recent developments, and had had the sudden and brilliant idea of pretending that Hector and Herbert had fallen through the grating accidentally and become imprisoned in the cellar through no fault of their own or his.

But the sight of the three figures in the hall took away his power of speech and, before he had recovered it, Mrs. Brown spoke in a firm voice.

"William, I'll ask you about this later. But for the present go down into the cellar at once and bring up those two children."

William obeyed. There was nothing else to do. He went down to the cellar and stopped the egg-battle.

"We've bombed the enemy," sang Hector, and:

"Is the war over now?" asked Herbert.

William assured them grimly that as far as they were concerned the war was over, and escorted them up the cellar stairs. Plastered with coal and egg they were still dimly recognisable as human beings. Miss Thompson pounced upon Herbert and took her hat trimming from his head.

"It'll need cleaning, of course," she said, examining it, "but I don't think it's damaged beyond repair."

Mrs. Monks fixed them with a stern eye.

"*Why* did you put carrots in my bag?" she said.

Then Ethel and Robert entered. They had just come

from their A.R.P. class. Ethel had been practising bandaging, and Robert had been listening to a lecture on decontamination.

There was a jagged cut on Hector's temple caused by an unusually resistant egg shell. It was exactly the size and shape of the cut on which Ethel had just been practising. She seized on him with gleaming eyes and began to hustle him upstairs.

"I don't know who you are," she said, "but I'm going to bandage that cut. Come on."

The last egg thrown at Herbert had evidently been a bad one. He stank to Heaven. . . . It was just such an object—blackened by smoke, soaked in noxious gases—on which Robert had imagined himself practising the art of decontamination.

"And I don't know who *you* are, but I'm going to decontaminate you."

"Yes!" said William bitterly, thinking of his own ill-fated attempt at A.R.P. work. "*They* c'n do it all right. No one stops *them*."

Mrs. Brown watched helplessly as Ethel and Robert swept the twins upstairs before them. The spirits of the twins were still undaunted.

"Aren't we having a lovely time, Hector?" said Herbert.

"Yes," said Hector happily. "I like wars."

Mrs. Brown watched till they were out of sight, then turned slowly to the spot from which William had spoken.

But William was no longer there.

William had decided that the time had come to try a spot of evacuation on his own account.

Chapter 2

William's Good-bye Present

"Uncle Paul's goin' back to Australia to-morrow," said Hubert Lane. "I'm goin' to see him off at Hadley Station. He says he'll call round an' say good-bye to you on the way."

"A'right," said William amicably.

There had been a lull in the hostilities between the Hubert Laneites and the Outlaws during the visit of Hubert's Uncle Paul from Australia. For Uncle Paul was an uncle after the Outlaws' own heart, and he evidently much preferred the Outlaws to his own nephew and his nephew's friends.

He had taken the Outlaws for long walks (Hubert didn't like long walks because they made him so breathless), shown them a new way of making fires, and initiated them into the lore of the bush. He could make whistles and carve toy boats with a few deft movements of the big clasp-knife he always carried in his pocket, and he could relate thrilling stories of true adventures that had been handed down to him from earlier settlers. Hubert Lane was not particularly interested in any of these things, but he realised that Uncle Paul was a social asset and began to put on even more airs than usual. The Outlaws restrained their natural reaction to this, and remained on outwardly friendly terms with him, for they were afraid that any open breach might deprive them of the precious company of Uncle Paul.

To William the visit had passed all too quickly. It had opened up whole new worlds of adventure, and he had proved an apt pupil at whistle and boat making. In fact, Uncle Paul had said that the last boat he had made was almost as good as he could have made himself.

"What you want," he had said, "is a good knife. I'll give you one before I go. I'll get you one like mine if I can."

"Like yours!" gasped William incredulously.

"Yes," said Uncle Paul, glancing carelessly at the magnificent weapon with which he had just fashioned a perfectly formed and perfectly balanced boat. "Those little penknives of yours are no good."

William had not yet received the clasp-knife, but he knew that Uncle Paul had not forgotten it.

"I've not forgotten that knife of yours," he had said the next day. "I went into Hadley about it, and they hadn't one in stock, but they're going to get one."

Though the last day of Uncle Paul's visit had arrived, and he had not yet had the knife, William did not feel the least uneasiness. Uncle Paul was not the sort of person who made promises, and then forgot them.

William was hanging about his front gate the next morning when the car containing Uncle Paul and Hubert came down the road on its way to Hadley Station. Beside Uncle Paul's bronze face and lean figure, Hubert looked more pallid and balloon-like than ever. He was smiling to himself as at some secret joke. Uncle Paul stopped the car and jumped out.

"I was coming to see you to say good-bye," he said to William. "We've had a great time together, haven't we? Don't forget what I told you about lighting fires. Your way was no good at all. And when you're tracking down wild animals be sure you're the right way of the wind, or they'll get your scent. And about that knife——"

"Yes?" said William eagerly.

"They said they'd have it in first thing this morning, so I'll stop the car at the shop in Hadley and get it, and Hubert here can bring it back to you. That'll be all right, won't it?"

"Yes," agreed William heartily, "an' I'm jolly grateful to you. I've wanted a knife like that all my life."

"Splendid!" said Uncle Paul. "That last boat you made was a fine one. I'm giving Hubert a pistol for his present. . . . Well, good-bye. See you again next time I'm over."

He drove off, Hubert still sitting beside him with that faint secret smile on his face.

William watched the car till it was out of sight. His sorrow at the departure of Uncle Paul was mingled with joy at the prospect of the possession of the magnificent clasp-knife. He hoped that Hubert would bring it straight back to him before going home. Then he remembered that curious smile on Hubert's face, and was conscious of a slight feeling of uneasiness. It wasn't a pleasant smile. He wondered what it meant.

His uneasiness increased as the morning passed by, and Hubert did not appear with the clasp-knife. After lunch he could restrain his impatience no longer and set out for the Lanes' house. Perhaps the shop hadn't got it to-day, after all. Perhaps he'd have to wait till to-morrow or even the day after. Well, he'd just have to wait, if that was the case. . . . but it was rotten of Hubert not to have come round to tell him.

Mrs. Lane happened to be passing through the hall when he knocked and came herself to the front door. She greeted him without enthusiasm. She was tired of seeing him about the place. Paul had encouraged him too much. She didn't know why Paul had wanted to have anything to do with a rough boy like that, when he'd got a dear, well-behaved boy like Hubert on the spot. He'd seemed sometimes—though she could hardly really believe this—to have actually preferred William to Hubert.

"Well?" she said coldly. "What do you want?"

"I've come for my knife," said William simply.

Mrs. Lane stared at him.

"Your what?" she said.

"My knife," said William. "The knife that Hubert's Uncle Paul's given Hubert for me."

"I don't know what you're talking about," said Mrs. Lane. "Hubert *has* a knife that his Uncle Paul gave him for a parting present, but I know nothing about any knife of yours. . . . Hubert!" she called.

Hubert came slowly into the hall. His fat pale face still wore the faint smile that it had worn earlier in the day when he had called at William's house with Uncle Paul.

"I've come for my knife," said William sternly.

The smile spread all over Hubert's fat, pale face.

"What knife?" he said.

"The knife Uncle Paul said he was giving you for me." Hubert took from his pocket an exact, but shiningly new, replica of Uncle Paul's clasp-knife. "Yes, that's it," said William eagerly.

But Hubert did not at once hand it over with apologies for the delay, as William expected him to. Instead, he slipped it back into his pocket with a careless air of proprietorship.

"That knife?" he said. "That's my knife. He gave it me for a good-bye present."

"He said he was giving you a pistol for a good-bye present," said William indignantly.

Hubert took out a shining new pistol from another pocket.

"IT IS MY KNIFE," SAID WILLIAM INDIGNANTLY. "UNCLE
PAUL TOLD ME HE WAS GOING TO GIVE IT TO ME."

"Yes," he smiled. "He gave me that, too."

William gazed at him blankly. He still couldn't believe
it. Surely even Hubert couldn't be guilty of such a mean
trick as that. . . .

"But he *promised* the knife to me," he insisted. "You

were there when he did. He said he'd call at the shop for it and give it you to give to me."

"He never did," said Hubert. "He never said anything about a knife when he called to say good-bye to you. He gave this knife to me, that's all I know."

William was, for a moment, struck speechless with horror, as he realised that Hubert actually meant to deny his rights to the knife. But even now he never doubted that immediate redress would be forthcoming from the grown-up world around. He turned indignantly to Mrs. Lane.

"It *is* my knife," he said. "Uncle Paul told me he was going to give it to me. He was goin' to call for it in Hadley this mornin', and give it to Hubert to give to me. He told me so. Hubert was there when he told me so."

Mrs. Lane looked at Hubert.

"Did he, Hubert?" she said.

Hubert met her eye blandly and unflinchingly.

"'Course he didn't," he said. "He's jus' makin' it all up to get the clasp-knife off me. Uncle Paul stopped the car in Hadley, same as I told you, an' went into this shop an' came out with the knife an' said: 'I want you to have this knife for a good-bye present, Hubert, as well as the pistol.' He said: 'I'd never dream of givin' a knife like this to that rotten ole William Brown.' An' I showed it to some boys in the village, an' they told William, I suppose, an' he's come round here tellin' lies to try an' get it off me."

William stared at him incredulously. He had lived for the moment when the precious knife should be his. He had thought of nothing, dreamed of nothing else. He couldn't believe that this was really happening.

"You *naughty* boy!" Mrs. Lane was saying to him. "How *dare* you come here with a string of lies like this?"

"But he did," said William desperately. "He gave it

me. He *did* give it me. *Honest* he did. He said he'd give it
to Hubert to give it to me——"

"Be quiet," interrupted Mrs. Lane severely. "If you
tell any more of these wicked lies I shall come round and
tell your father this evening. Of *course* I believe Hubert
rather than you. Hubert's a most truthful little boy,
aren't you, Hubert?"

"Yes, Mother," agreed Hubert smugly.

"So go away at once, William Brown, and I hope that
Hubert will never have anything more to do with you
after this."

Even William, practised orator as he was, knew that
further protestation would be useless. Hubert had stepped back behind his mother and was holding up the
clasp-knife with a grimace of jeering triumph. William
restrained himself with difficulty, and turned to go
slowly down to the gate. He heard Mrs. Lane say,
"You're never to speak to that wicked boy again,
Hubert," before she shut the door. (He thought grimly
that Hubert would be only too ready to obey that
particular injunction just now.) He walked down the
road, still stunned and bewildered by what had happened. It wasn't only the loss of the longed-for knife,
though that, in itself, was a crushing blow. It was the
meanness of the trick by which Hubert had gained
possession of it. It was incredible that such a trick should
succeed, and yet, the more William thought about it, the
more difficult it seemed to circumvent it. Uncle Paul
himself was now well on the way to Australia, and
appeal to him was impossible. Appeal to Hubert's
mother had been tried and had failed. Appeal to his own
parents would be equally useless. They would probably
believe his story rather than Hubert's (though he had
carefully concealed Uncle Paul's promises of his knife
from them till now, fearing lest, with their strange

prejudice against such weapons, they should ask him to change the gift for something else), but, in face of Mrs. Lane's firm belief in her own son, they would not be able to insist on his handing it over to William. William, indeed, was afraid that his parents would treat the whole affair with that callous indifference with which grown-ups usually treat burning questions of right and wrong. To take it from Hubert by force also was impossible. Mrs. Lane—or, worse still, Mr. Lane—would come round to see his parents, and retribution, as well as the return of the knife to Hubert, would surely follow.

He walked gloomily on to the old barn where he had arranged to meet the Outlaws to show them his precious new possession. As soon as they saw him they knew that something was wrong. Not thus—slowly, dejectedly, thoughtfully—does the owner of a brand-new clasp-knife walk. They leapt at once to the natural conclusion that the knife had not arrived in time. Even a day's—even half an hour's—delay in such a case would be a bitter disappointment.

"Haven't you got it?" called Ginger as he approached.

"No," said William.

"Never mind," Ginger encouraged him. "My mother ordered somethin' in Hadley last week, an' it hadn't come the mornin' they said it would have come, but it came in the afternoon an' she got it at tea-time. I bet it'll have come before to-night."

"Oh, it's come," said William bitterly. "It's come all right."

They stared at him in astonishment. Why wasn't he swaggering, then? Why wasn't he displaying it? Why did he wear this tragic mien?

"Where is it, then?" demanded Douglas.

"*He's* got it," said William.

"Who?"

"Hubert Lane," said William, spitting the name out as if it were some noxious draught.

They crowded round him in consternation as he told them the whole story. At first, like him, they were incredulous. They couldn't believe that such a thing could happen in a universe that was supposed to be founded more or less on principles of justice and equity. Their minds, as William's had done, turned instinctively to the tribunal of the grown-up world. Hubert's mother . . . Uncle Paul . . . William's mother. They could not believe, till William pointed it out, that appeal to these quarters would be useless.

"We'll take it off him, then," said Ginger decisively.

"Yes," said William bitterly, "an' have it took back and everyone mad at us on top of it."

With this, too, they had reluctantly to agree, and, after half an hour's futile discussion, they parted despondently, overwhelmed and aghast at the horror of the situation and their utter inability to deal with it. William, without much hope, approached his parents, and their attitude was what he had expected it to be. They believed him implicitly, accorded him a certain perfunctory sympathy, but were obviously relieved that Fate had sent the clasp-knife to another home.

"I'm sorry about it, dear," said his mother, "but of course, we can't do anything, and, really, when one remembers the damage you did with that scout's knife——"

"That was over a year ago," protested William indignantly. "I'm a good deal older than that now. An', anyway, I didn't really mean to cut that table in the drawing-room. I was only tryin' if the blade was really sharp."

His father dismissed the matter with a careless "One

must learn to bear these little disappointments, my boy, without making a fuss"—an attitude that William felt to be wholly inadequate to the occasion.

At first he hoped that Hubert might wreak such havoc with the clasp-knife in the Lane home, that Mrs. Lane would take it from him and give it to William, but in this he was doomed to disappointment. Hubert had no real use for the clasp-knife. He was definitely not a clasp-knife boy. He had taken so much trouble to obtain it only because William wanted it, and he wanted to "score off" William. The pleasure he got out of it—and it was a very real pleasure to him—was in hanging out of his bedroom window, safe from attack, and displaying it to William and the Outlaws with jeering triumph whenever they passed down the road in front of his house. His pistol he played with quite often, but it was the clasp-knife that gave him most satisfaction.

It was just when William had almost given up hope of either getting back his knife or avenging the insult, that an idea occurred to him. He remembered quite suddenly the weak spot in Hubert's armour. Hubert still believed in fairies and witches and spells. There had been an historic occasion when he had even managed to persuade Hubert that he had been made invisible. Surely that weakness could be turned to account now. . . . He called a meeting of the Outlaws in the old barn, and together they formed a Plan.

Hubert, meantime, had also formed a Plan. Since acquiring the clasp-knife he had not dared to adventure his precious person among the Outlaws. He knew, of course, that any attack upon him would meet with prompt vengeance at the hands of his parents, but, though he enjoyed the thought of the vengeance, he shrank from the thought of the attack that must precede it. He was tired of the refuge of his house and garden, and wanted to go further afield, so he had thought out a Plan to trick the Outlaws into friendly relations with him in spite of the clasp-knife episode.

The next morning, therefore, when he saw William and Ginger in the road below, he leaned out of his window and hailed them in an obviously propitiatory fashion.

"I say," he said, "I'm goin' to have a party soon. There's goin' to be a trifle an' four different kinds of jelly, all with cream on 'em. Would you like to come?"

He had, of course, no intention of having a party, or of asking the Outlaws to it, even if he had one, but he was stupid enough to judge everyone by himself, and he took it for granted that the Outlaws would swallow any affront for the sake of a trifle and four different kinds of jelly with cream on. Ordinarily, the overture would merely have hardened the Outlaws' hostility, but on this occasion they were secretly delighted. The one obstacle to their Plan had been the difficulty, in the present circumstances, of establishing relations with Hubert (it was for that purpose that William and Ginger had come to the house), and Hubert himself had solved it. They stood in the road and looked up at him.

"Can we really come?" said William assuming a nauseating pleasant expression.

"'Course you can," said Hubert, sniggering to himself at the success of his ruse. "All of you can come. We're goin' to have cream buns with chocolates on, too," he invented glibly.

Ginger imitated William's nauseous expression.

"Oo, how lovely!" he gushed. "It's awfully kind of you, Hubert, isn't it?" appealing to William.

"Oo, isn't it!" said William, and they both turned glassy grins up to Hubert.

Their performance was neither natural nor convinc-

ing, and anyone less self-centred than Hubert would
have suspected it at once. But Hubert was so taken up by
his own cleverness that he accepted it at its face value.

"Will you come out an' play with us, Hubert?" said
William.

Again Hubert sniggered secretly at the exquisite joke.
Here they were, ready to lick his shoes in their eagerness
to be invited to his party, and there wasn't going to be a
party at all! They'd forgotten all about the clasp-knife
(as he knew they would) in their excitement at the
prospect of the (purely imaginary) trifles and jellies and
cream buns.

"Come and play with us, Hubert," pleaded Ginger.
"We've gotter secret. We've not told anyone else yet.
We'll tell you if you'll come."

Next to greed, Hubert's consuming passion was curiosity. They knew that he would now have no peace of
mind till he had learnt the secret.

"All right," he said condescendingly. "I'll come
along. . . ."

He vanished from the window and soon appeared at
the gate.

"It's all right about that knife, Hubert," William
greeted him pacifically. "You can keep it."

"Thought you'd feel that way," said Hubert with an
unpleasant sneer, "when you knew there was goin' to be
a party." He took out the knife from one pocket, the
pistol from another, flourished them carelessly before
the Outlaws' eyes, then restored them to his pockets.

Once more the Outlaws restrained themselves with
difficulty. They walked together down the road, Hubert
dilating on the gastronomical treat in store for those who
were fortunate enough to be invited to his party.

They reached the field by the old barn. William and
Ginger led him across the stile into the field. He looked

"I'M GOIN' TO HAVE A PARTY SOON," SAID HUBERT.
"WOULD YOU LIKE TO COME?"

round with his superior sneer.

"Well," he said condescendingly, "what's this secret of yours?"

"It's this," said William, lowering his voice confidentially. "When we came here this morning we saw an ole woman in the field with a cloak an' a big pointed hat an' a broomstick."

The superior sneer fell from Hubert's face.

"It was a witch," he said excitedly. "It was a witch, of course. What was she doin'?"

"She was jus' goin' about an' wavin' her broomstick an' sayin' things."

"Spells!" said Hubert, his round, credulous face pink with eagerness. "She was makin' spells. I say"—his eyes glinted greedily—"did she say anythin' about findin' treasure or anythin' like that?"

Walking by his side, William carefully led him on to a

spot that had recently been burnt brown by one of the Outlaws' camp-fires.

"She said somethin' over that bit you're walkin' on now," he said reflectively.

"What was it?" said Hubert anxiously.

"Well, it went somethin' like this," said William.

" 'Whoever treads upon this bit of burned,
    Into a hen-coop shall his home be turned.'

"And then it went on somethin' about all the family that was in the house should be turned into hens, an' anyone of the family who wasn't in it when the spell came on should be turned into hens the minute they saw the hen-coop."

"CAN WE REALLY COME?" SAID WILLIAM.

Hubert's mouth dropped open in sudden dismay, and he leapt quickly away from the patch of burnt grass.

"W-w-w-what?" he stammered. "A hen-coop?"

"Yes," said William carelessly, "but I don't suppose there's really anythin' in it. Go'n' look if your house is turned into a hen-coop. You can see from the stile, can't you?"

Hubert started forward, then remembered the second part of the spell, and returned.

"I'd better not," he said anxiously. "You go 'n' look," he added, turning to Ginger.

Ginger went down to the stile, from which he could see the solid, foursquare structure of stone and brick that was the Lanes' house.

"Corks!" he ejaculated in well-simulated horror. "It's gone. There's only a hen-coop."

Hubert paled.

"I don't b'lieve you," he stammered. "I d-d-d-don't believe you."

"Well, come and look for yourself," challenged Ginger.

Again Hubert remembered the latter part of the spell, and shook his head.

"No, I won't," he said. "You want to get me turned into a hen, too, that's what you want. . . . Anyway, I don't believe you."

"Well, come and look for yourself if you don't believe me."

"No, I won't."

"Well, it's true."

"I bet it isn't."

"Well, come and look for yourself."

"No, I won't."

Matters having thus reached a deadlock, Douglas

appeared sauntering idly from behind the old barn. A wink from William told him that the Plan was, so far, going according to programme.

"I say, Hubert," said Douglas airily, "what's happened to your house?"

Hubert turned greener than ever at this confirmation of his fears.

"W-w-w-what?" he stammered.

"It's gone," said Douglas. "I've just passed it now an' it's gone, an' there's a hen-coop where it was, with a brown an' white hen scratchin' about outside it."

That was a clever touch of verisimilitude on Douglas's part. He had seen Mrs. Lane through the window as he passed the house, and she had been wearing a brown and white dress.

"Corks! That'll be Mother," said Hubert, his eyes growing rounder and rounder with horror.

"I say, there's a hen jus' settin' off from the coop an' going down the road," called Ginger from the stile.

"That'll be Father," moaned Hubert. "He goes to the station about this time."

"I bet they won't let him on the train," said Ginger. "Not like that."

Henry appeared suddenly in the road, vaulted the stile and ran up to join William and Douglas and Hubert. He evidently had some exciting news to impart.

"I say!" he said. "Hubert's house has gone. There's jus' a hen-coop there."

At this proof from yet another and (as it seemed) independent source, Hubert burst into tears. They crowded round, comforting him.

"Don't worry, Hubert. They have quite a good time, hens."

"You'll get to like worms an' grubs after a bit, I expect."

"You'd better go back an' get turned into one now an' get it over. You'll have to, sooner or later, you know. You'll get used to it. I'll try'n' stop Jumble chasin' you when we pass your coop."

"I expect you're hungry aren't you, Hubert? You'd better go home an' have some nice grubs an' worms. You have to eat a lot of dirt with 'em, but you'll soon get used to it."

"You'll soon get used to the funny way they have to drink, too."

"I bet you'll get a bit tired at first, havin' to sleep on one leg, but it won't seem so bad after a year or two."

"I believe he's turning into one now, don't you? His face is gettin' jus' like a hen's."

Hubert's sobs turned into long howls.

"I d-d-don't want to be a h-h-hen," he yelled. "I d-d-d-don't want to be a h-h-h-h-hen."

"Well, listen, Hubert," said William kindly. "I heard this witch say somethin' else after she'd said that about the hens. . . ."

Hubert stopped howling and turned a tear-stained face to William.

"W-what did she say?" he asked.

"Well," said William, "she went over to the stream here"—they followed him to the ditch at the edge of the field—"an' she waved her broomstick over it an' she said:

> " 'An' never shall he be free of the spell
> Till he throws into here somethin' that cuts an'
>   somethin' that shoots as well.' "

Hubert blinked and considered. Then he plunged his hand into his pocket and brought out the clasp-knife.

"D'you think that'd do?" he said anxiously.

William examined it with a judicial air.

"It might," he said, as if a little uncertain. "It cuts anyway. No harm in tryin'. But what about the other? She said 'Somethin' that shoots as well'."

From another pocket Hubert brought out his pistol.

"What about this?" he said. "Would this do?"

"You might try," said William doubtfully. "Try throwin' 'em both in together. Come on. Throw 'em. One, two, *three*!"

Pistol and penknife fell with a splash into the little stream. At once Ginger raised a cry from the stile.

"I say!" he said. "Hubert's house has come back. That hen-coop's gone, an' Hubert's house has come back."

Hubert's fat, tear-stained face shone with relief.

"Corks!" he said. "I'm jolly glad you heard her say that end bit."

"She said somethin' else," said William. "She said that if ever you came here to look for 'em in the stream, or if ever you told anyone about this hen business you'd be turned into somethin' a jolly sight worse than a hen."

Hubert paled again.

"I won't," he said earnestly. "I jolly well won't. . . . I promise I won't. . . . I say!"—uneasily—"I don't look as if I was turnin' into a hen now, do I?"

"No," William reassured him. "You're gone quite back to a boy again now."

It was with the greatest difficulty, however, that they prevailed upon Hubert to go home. All four had to go in turn to the stile and assure him again and again that the hen-coop had vanished and the house was standing there as before.

"It'll be quite all right now with you havin' thrown those things into the stream," William assured him again. "They've broke the spell. An' I'll dig up that bit of burnt grass so that no one else can go on it.''

Cautiously, fearfully, his face green with apprehension, Hubert approached the stile. Then he gave a whoop of joy.

"It *has* come back," he said exultantly. "It's all right. It *has* come back."

"Well, don't you forget about not tellin' anyone," William warned him.

"No, I won't," said Hubert fervently, "and I'm jolly grateful to you for rememberin' the end part, the part that turned it back. Worms!" He gave a shudder of disgust. "I was jolly well dreadin' havin' to eat *worms*."

"You'd better not say anythin' to your mother," said William. "She won't remember havin' been a hen. They never do once the spell's off."

"I know," said Hubert. "No, I won't say anythin' to her. I say, I'm *jolly* glad it's turned back. Did it go quite sudden?" he asked Ginger.

"Yes," said Ginger. "Quite sudden. One minute it was a hen-coop, an' the next it was a house again.'

"Well, I'm goin' home, then," said Hubert. "I'm jolly hungry. Worms!" he said again with a grimace, and set off at his fat, slow trot down the road towards the house.

*   *   *

The next morning, as he was standing at the gate, the Outlaws passed him. William held the clasp-knife and Ginger the pistol. Neither had been damaged by its brief immersion in the stream. Hubert looked at them with interest.

"Where did you get those?" he said.

William turned a bland, expressionless face to him.

"The fairies gave them us," he said.

Chapter 3

William's Day Off

"They're comin' for four days," said Ginger. "They're slum children. They've never seen a cow or anything like that."

"Well, there's not much to see in a cow," said William judicially. "I'd as soon not see one as see one. You can't have any fun with a cow. I've tried."

"Well, they've not seen fields or woods, either. Only streets an' suchlike."

"That's jolly hard lines," admitted William. "Where did you say they were comin'?"

"To Eastbrook Farm. Mrs. Camp's havin' them. They're sent by some sort of soci'ty what pays for slum children to come into the country."

"Well, I vote we take 'em round a bit an' show 'em woods an' cows an' things," said William.

"Miss Milton's sister's havin' 'em to tea the first day," put in Henry. "I heard my mother say so this mornin'."

"Corks!" said William, aghast. "Fancy them havin' to waste an afternoon goin' to *her*!" Miss Milton had lent her cottage to her sister for the summer, and, though William had not yet met the lady, he had received the discouraging news that she was an almost exact replica of her sister. "They must be jolly potty to want to go to tea with *her*. . . ."

"Well, they don't know what she's like," said Ginger. "They prob'ly think she's goin' to give 'em a jolly good time."

"A jolly good time!" echoed William in a tone of withering sarcasm. "*Her!* Not much good time about *her*! She'll want 'em to sit round while she talks about the weather. They'd be a jolly sight better off in the slums."

The Outlaws would probably have devised some plan for the rescue of the slum children from Miss Milton then and there, had not the news been brought to them that Hubert Lane had some piebald mice for sale at a shilling each. They had been bought for him by one of his adoring aunts as a parting present at the end of a visit and, as Hubert did not care for mice, he was offering them for sale. It happened that by little short of a miracle the Outlaws could scrape a shilling together. Henry had received threepence recently from his mother for looking after his young sister in the garden for an hour while she and the nurse were busy. ("Yes, an' it was more worth three pounds than threepence," said Henry darkly. "I was wore out with crawling about with her on my back round an' round the lawn. Seems to think I'm a slave 'stead of a yuman bein'.") Douglas had been given threepence by his father for finding a fountain-pen that he had lost. (Douglas, who had "borrowed" the pen and forgotten to return it, "found" it by the simple process of bringing it down from his bedroom.) Ginger had discovered how to pick the lock of his money-box and had taken out the three pennies that were its sole occupants, and William had sold a collection of "trained" caterpillars, vaunted to be of surpassing intelligence, to a credulous and wealthy school friend also for the sum of threepence.

They set off light-heartedly down the road to Hubert Lane's house. The feud with the Hubert Laneites was temporarily in abeyance, and the Outlaws took for granted that relations were sufficiently stabilised for ordinary commercial purposes.

They knocked with resounding confidence at the Lane front door.

A maid answered the knock, stared at them morosely, and fetched Hubert. Hubert looked a little apprehensive when he saw the four Outlaws clustered on the doorstep.

"What d'you want?" he said.

William held out the twelve pennies in a hot, grubby hand.

"Can we have one of your mice, please?" he said.

A slow smile spread over Hubert's face. Here was a blessed opportunity to thwart his hated foes. Moreover, he was on his own ground, and no harm could come to him.

"No, you can't," he said.

"But—someone said you were sellin' 'em," said William indignantly.

"Yes, I am," said Hubert, "but not to you."

The Outlaws stared at him in amazement.

"But—we've got a shillin'," said Ginger.

Hubert retreated into the hall so as to be well under the protection of his own roof tree.

"Don't care if you've got ten shillin's," he said. "D'you think I'd sell one of my piebald mice to *you*? *You're* not goin' to have one of my piebald mice, an' I'm jolly glad you want one of them so's you can't have it. See? *Yah!*"

William stepped forward instinctively to accept this challenge, but Hubert vanished into the drawing-room, and almost at once Mrs. Lane appeared in his place, looking so fierce that the Outlaws instinctively turned tail and fled down the road. Derisive shouts from Hubert followed them.

"Think I'd let you have one of my piebald mice? I'd let anyone on earth have 'em 'cept you. I'd *give* 'em away rather than let you buy 'em. *Yah!*"

The Outlaws walked on, hot with anger and humiliation.

"Well, I like that!" exploded William. "I jolly well like that. We'd got a shillin' same as anyone else. He'd said he was sellin' 'em for a shillin'. I bet it's against the lor not to sell a thing you've *said* you were sellin'."

"I bet it is," agreed Ginger. "Anyway, we don't want his rotten ole piebald mice."

"No, we jolly well don't want his rotten ole piebald mice," agreed the others.

But they were disappointed and humiliated none the less. They *did* want a piebald mouse, and even more than the loss of that was their public humiliation at the hands of their foe.

"He'll tell everyone," said Henry morosely. "He'll tell everyone we came an' asked for one an' he wouldn't sell us one."

"Let's get someone to buy it for us," suggested Douglas, "then he won't know it's us buyin' it."

But this scheme did not appeal to William's proud spirit.

"No, that's not the same," he said. "The thing is to make him sell *us* one."

"We might get in his house somehow," suggested Ginger, "an' pinch one of 'em an' leave a shillin' in its place."

"No, *that* wouldn't do," said William. "He's gotter sell it us an' everyone's gotter know he's sold it us."

"How're you goin' to make him?" demanded Ginger.

"I don't know yet," said William.

He cogitated the problem at intervals during the rest of the day without arriving at any decision, and the next morning the news of the arrival of the two slum children at Eastbrook Farm drove the whole question out of his mind.

The Outlaws went over to the farm immediately on receiving the news, in order to inspect the newcomers. They found two boys standing by the farm gate wearing grey shorts and grey jerseys with large blue and white badges. They looked very clean and very bored. Greetings were exchanged—cautious and a little defiant on both sides. The newcomers, it turned out, were called Bert and Syd. They were ten and eleven years old. No, they didn't think much of the country so far. A goat had butted them and a gander had chased them. They were obviously disillusioned and homesick.

"You come along with us," suggested William, "an' we'll show you some of our places."

Bert and Syd brightened. Mr. and Mrs. Camp were well-meaning but preoccupied. The prospect of playmates of their own age was enlivening. They felt less oppressively like strangers in a strange land.

"Don't mind if we do," agreed Bert cautiously.

Bert was the older and obviously the leading spirit. He had a slight cast in one eye that lent him a somewhat sardonic aspect, and a more than slight suggestion of adenoids. Syd was small and gingery and obviously ready to follow Bert's lead unquestioningly wherever it took him.

"Don't mind if we do," he repeated.

They accompanied the Outlaws to the main road and

across the fields to the woods. They were at first inclined to be aggressive, and to belittle such aspects of the countryside as the Outlaws pointed out to them, but their hostility soon melted in the warmth of the Outlaws' friendliness. The Outlaws, on their side, felt, as it were, on their mettle to prove the superiority of their own

"YOU COME ALONG WITH US," SUGGESTED WILLIAM, "AN' WE'LL SHOW YOU SOME OF OUR PLACES."

surroundings to those from which Bert and Syd had come, and soon the six of them were happily engaged in a rough and tumble game in the wood. Bert and Syd were quick to enter into the spirit of it, and proved themselves a sufficiently sporting couple.

Next they went to the old barn, made a fire, and cooked one of the Outlaws' famous extempore meals, consisting of oddments purloined from their households' larders—in this case, a sardine, a piece of sponge cake, a cold sausage, a tinned apricot, a handful of cold

"DON'T MIND IF WE DO," AGREED BERT CAUTIOUSLY.

porridge, and a pennyworth of sherbet. This was well mixed together, generously laced with liquorice water, and heated in the treasured saucepan that Ginger's mother's cook had given him when it became unfit for household use. Bert and Syd ate their share manfully and pronounced it excellent. They contributed their part, too, to the general entertainment. They were members of a street gang at home and had stories of adventure to relate that made even the Outlaws, seasoned daredevils as they were, hold their breath with excitement. They displayed, too, as they unthawed, a dry and caustic wit that delighted their hosts. The six returned to the farm firm friends.

"Tell you what we'll do this afternoon," said William. "We'll go over to Marleigh. There's some caves there an' we can play smugglers."

The faces of Bert and Syd had lightened at the suggestion, but suddenly they clouded over as a memory occurred to them.

"Coo!" said Bert regretfully. "I don't 'arf wish we could, but we can't. We've gotter go to tea somewhere this afternoon."

"A Miss Milton, or sumpthin'," supplemented Syd.

"You'll have a jolly dull time there," William prophesied. "She's awful."

"She won't even give you a decent tea if she's anythin' like her sister," said Ginger.

"She's worse than her sister," said Douglas gloomily. "I've seen her."

"Fancy havin' to waste an afternoon on *her*!" said William sympathetically.

"I bet we could get you a jolly good tea, come to that," said Ginger. "Our cook's made gingerbread this mornin', an' I bet she'd let me have some for you."

"An' I bet I could get some of our iced cake," said Henry. "It's orange icing, an' it's jolly good."

"Yes. . . . But Mrs. Camp'll make us go, I expect," said Bert.

"An' ole Miss What-ever-she's-called'll come an' fetch us if we don't," put in Syd gloomily.

"S'pose she will," said Ginger, "but it seems a jolly shame."

"A whole bloomin' afternoon," groaned Bert.

"Out of only four bloomin' days," added Syd.

Their eyes turned to William. On William's face was a faraway look that was well known to the Outlaws. It was obvious that one of his Ideas was slowly dawning on the horizon of his mind.

"I say . . ." he began.

"Well?" said the others expectantly.

"S'pose two of us pretend to be Bert an' Syd an' go to tea to old Miss Milton's 'stead of them? It doesn't matter much for us, 'cause we can go to Marleigh caves any day, but they've only got four days an' it might rain on the others."

For a moment their expressions brightened, then gloom closed over them again.

"She's seen me," said Ginger. "I met her when I was out with my mother yesterday." A look of disgust came over his face at the memory as he continued, "She said she hoped I liked school, an' was workin' hard at my lessons."

"She's seen me, too," said Douglas. "She came to our house yesterday, an' every time I said a word she said that little boys oughter be seen and not heard."

"An' she's seen me, too," said Henry. "I was jus' walkin' past her house whistlin' to myself an' sort of hittin' the hedge with a stick without thinkin', an' she came out, mad as mad, and said if I did it again she'd tell the police."

The faces of Bert and Syd fell at this recital.

"Crikey!" said Bert. "It's goin' to be a bloomin' fine tea-party."

"Not 'arf," agreed Syd bitterly.

"But she's not seen me," said William. "Tell you what. . . . I'll say I'm Bert an' that Syd's gotter cold or somethin'. An' then you can all go off to Marleigh caves, an' I'll go 'n' have tea with her, an' she'll never know it's not you, an' you won't have wasted all that time on her."

"Coo!" said Bert. "That's jolly decent of you."

"Not 'arf," agreed Syd.

The others looked a little doubtful.

"Are you *sure* she's not seen you?" said Ginger.

"I bet you can't keep it up," said Douglas.

"You'll only make a mess of it," prophesied Henry.

"'Course I'm sure she's not seen me," said William impatiently. "An', anyway, I'll make myself look different same as actors an' detectives do."

"*They* wear beards," said Ginger. "You can't wear a beard."

"I'm not goin' to wear a beard," said William testily. "I'm jus' goin' to make my face different. That's all they do. They jus' make their faces diff'rent."

"Don't see how you *could* make yours look diff'-rent," said Ginger, looking critically at that uncompromising member.

"What d'you mean by that?" challenged William.

"Nothin'," said Ginger pacifically. "I di'n' say there was anythin' wrong with it. I only said you couldn't make it different."

"I bet I can," said William. "I can pull better faces than you, anyway."

"Yes, but you can't keep a face pulled for hours an' hours an' eat an' drink with it pulled. Not even *you* could. You're only a yuman bein' same as everyone else."

"Oh, go on," said William sarcastically. "Go on makin' objections. I tell you, you've always gotter take a risk in an adventure. It's not an adventure if you don't take a risk in it. Well, my face is my risk an' I bet I can take it all right."

"We're dressed diff'rent, too," said Bert, looking from his jersey to William's coat.

"Well, we can change, can't we?" said William serenely, for opposition was having its usual effect of hardening his purpose. "You all go on makin' objections an' objections to every little thing. What would people in hist'ry've done if they'd all been like you? There'd have been no one to follow those great generals same as Magna Charta an' suchlike."

"Well, we aren't in hist'ry," said Douglas, ignoring the doubtful historical allusion.

"No, but I've always wanted to be," said William. "I bet I'd've been as good as anyone there. I bet I'd've managed to blow up that ole Crystal Palace better than Guy Fawkes did."

"It wasn't the Crystal Palace," said Henry.

"Oh, shut up!" said the exasperated William. "I'm sick of talkin' an' talkin' an' talkin'." He turned to Bert. "Would you rather go to tea to Miss Milton, or to Marleigh caves?"

"*Me?* Crikey!" said Bert. "Marleigh caves, of course."

"Not 'arf," agreed Syd.

"Right, then," said William in a business-like voice. "We'll all meet at the ole barn an' you an' me'll change clothes an' you can go to Marleigh caves."

"Good egg!" cried Bert and Syd simultaneously.

* * *

William walked slowly and purposefully towards Miss
Milton's house, intent upon the manipulation of his
face. He was representing Bert's slight cast by his best
squint—a squint brought to perfection by years of practice. He did it by opening his eyes to their fullest extent
and fixing them on the end of his nose. Bert's suggestion
of adenoids he represented by opening his mouth loosely
to the size of a ping-pong ball. In order further to
disguise himself he had damped his hair and brushed it
into a straight fringe just above his eyes, and was walking
with a curious, stooping, shambling gait, letting his
hands dangle about his knees. It was not surprising that a
nervous and elderly lady, who had just got off the 'bus,
having come from a considerable distance in order to
inspect the brasses in the church should, after one
startled glance at him, get back on to the 'bus and go
home again. Even Miss Milton, redoubtable warrior as
she was, blenched slightly as she saw the figure that was
shambling slowly up to her front door. William, aware of
her scrutiny from the drawing-room window, intensified
the squint, opened his mouth yet further, and dangled
his hands more violently. Miss Milton herself came to
the door.

"Please, mum," began William in a deep, throaty
voice, before she could speak. (Bert had handed on to
him all Mrs. Camp's directions as to behaviour. "Mind
you call her 'Mum', now, an' be respectful.") "Please,
mum, I'm Bert, an' Syd couldn't come. He's gotter bad
cold."

He opened his eyes to their utmost capacity and fixed
them with all his might on the end of his nose. He was
finding his squint useful. It saved him from the necessity
of meeting Miss Milton's eye.

"I'm sorry to hear that," said Miss Milton, conscientiously trying to overcome the distaste that his appearance inspired in her. "Come in, dear boy. Wipe your feet well on the mat and then come into the drawing-room."

William followed her into the drawing-room and sat down on a small chair by the window. One of Mrs. Camp's admonitions had been: "Don't speak till you're spoken to." William found this advice useful as the upkeep of squint and ping-pong ball mouth demanded his full attention.

Miss Milton looked at him, blinked, looked away, then, summoning all her courage, looked at him again.

"Are you enjoying your holiday in the country?" she said.

"Yes, mum," said William in the deep, throaty voice.

"I suppose you've never been in the country before, have you?"

"No, mum."

"It must be a delightful experience for you."

"Yes, mum."

"I suppose that badge is the badge of the society that sends you out into the country like this?"

"Yes, mum," said William, without removing his squint to look at it.

"I hope you realise that you're a very lucky boy."

"Yes, mum."

Miss Milton tried to think of something else to say, but failed.

"Perhaps," she said at last, "you'd like to come out and see the garden, would you?"

"Yes, mum," said William.

He followed her out into the little garden.

"It's my sister's garden really, of course," said Miss Milton, "and she likes to keep it tidy, so don't go on to the grass. There's plenty of room for you to walk on the path."

William was tired of saying "Yes, mum". He was artist enough to want to make more of his part than that.

"Grass, mum?" he said in his deep, throaty voice. "What's grass?"

Miss Milton was taken aback for a moment. Surely even slum children knew what grass was. But evidently they didn't, so she hastened to explain.

"That's grass," she said, pointing to her sister's sparse little lawn. "It's—well, it's just grass," she ended lamely.

William began to feel that a certain amount of enjoyment might, after all, be extracted from the situation.

He pointed over the hedge to a cow that was pleasantly ruminating in the next field.

"What's that?" he gruffed.

"That's a cow."

"What's a cow?"

Miss Milton sighed. But, of course, it was quite natural that a slum child should never have seen a cow.

"It's—just a cow, dear," she said. "A cow is—well, it's a cow."

Miss Milton's cat sauntered out of the kitchen door and eyed William sardonically.

"What's that?' he said, pointing at it.

"A cat, of course," said Miss Milton rather sharply. "Surely you've seen cats at home."

William realised that he was rather overdoing his town-bred ignorance.

"It's bigger than town cats," he said hastily.

"I suppose it is," said Miss Milton, appeased.

The cat, who had recognised William, winked at him and went indoors again.

Miss Milton told him the names of the various flowers as they went round the garden.

"That's a viola, dear, and that's a campanula, and that's an antirrhinum. . . ."

William thought wistfully of Marleigh caves and wished that he was there with the others.

"And now, dear," said Miss Milton, ending her recital. "It's time we went in to tea."

William resisted the temptation to say, "What's tea?" and instead pointed to a thrush that was sitting on the top of a hedge and said: "What's that?"

"A thrush, dear," said Miss Milton, trying to be patient.

"What's a thrush?" said William.

"Just a bird like any other bird. You've surely seen birds before. Our little feathered friends who—er—who sing."

"Why?" said William, who thought that Miss Milton might at any rate pay for the boredom she was inflicting on him.

"What do you mean, 'why'?"

"Why do they sing?"

"Well—er—why does anyone sing?" countered Miss Milton.

"Well, why do they?" said William.

"Because they—well, really, my dear boy, that's a very silly question. They—they just sing. It's a God-given gift."

"Same as cats an' donkeys?"

"No, those haven't nice voices at all."

"Who gives 'em *them*, then?" enquired William.

Miss Milton pretended not to hear. "Now tea, dear," she said brightly, leading the way into the dining-room.

It was, as Ginger had prophesied, a rotten tea. There

was a small plate of sparsely buttered bread, a plate of plain, unbuttered buns, and a few stale Marie biscuits.

William soon emptied the plates, but Miss Milton did not have them refilled.

"I'm glad you've made such a good tea," she said. She looked at him with shrinking interest. "I suppose you've seen an oculist about your—er—squint?"

"Yes," said William, hastily doing it again. He'd been forgetting it since he started his tea. "He said there was no cure."

"It seems to come and go in such an odd way," went on Miss Milton, fascinated and repelled by the phenomenon.

"Yes," agreed William. "He said that sort couldn't ever be cured."

"Really? Of course," she admitted. "I don't know much about the subject. It's very bad just now, isn't it?" as William did a particularly ferocious one.

"Yes," agreed William, and added hopefully, "It comes on worst when I'm hungry."

"But you've just had your tea," said Miss Milton.

William made no comment on this.

"Well, just stay here a moment," went on Miss Milton. "I'll try to get a little companion of your own age. You'd like that, wouldn't you?"

William grunted non-committally, and she went into the hall. He followed her to the door to listen. She was telephoning to Mrs. Lane.

"I've got one of those slum children from Eastbrook Farm to tea, and he's absolutely hopeless. A dreadful squint and almost mental. I wondered if your dear little Hubert would come along and give me a hand with entertaining him. . . . You'll send him round at once?

How kind of you! We'll expect him in a few minutes, then."

She returned to William, who had gone back to his chair and assumed his most devastating squint.

"A very nice and well-behaved little boy I know is coming round to see you, Bert," she said. "I don't approve of rough games, but there isn't any reason why he shouldn't take you for a nice quiet walk down the road and show you some—er—cows and things."

William squinted at her in wild desperation.

"I think p'raps I'd better be goin' home now," he said.

"Oh, but Mrs. Camp said you needn't go till six," objected Miss Milton.

"Yes, but—but," with sudden inspiration, "what with Syd ill I think p'raps I'd better be gettin' back."

"If there's any cause for anxiety," said Miss Milton, "I'll come along with you and see how he is."

"Oh, no," said William hastily. "No, he's not as bad as that."

"Well, then, dear, I think it would do you good to meet this boy who's coming. He's a very nice boy, and it would be a privilege for you to know him. As I said, he can take you a little walk and show you the country. Birds and things."

William was on the point of inventing a sudden illness of his own, when he saw Hubert entering the garden gate. Escape was now impossible. He sat there, intensifying his squint, and opening his mouth to the size of a cricket ball.

Miss Milton went to the door and returned followed by Hubert. Hubert looked at William and recognition leapt into his eyes, then died away again. The boy had looked like William Brown at first sight, but on further inspection he obviously wasn't. His clothes were different. His hair was different. His mouth was different. His eyes were different.

"This is Bert," Miss Milton introduced him, "and this, Bert, is Hubert. . . . Now, Hubert, I want you to take Bert a nice quiet walk down the road and show him the country. You'll go with Hubert, won't you, Bert?"

"Yes, mum," said William in his deep, throaty voice.

(His voice was different, too, thought Hubert.)

"Come back in a quarter of an hour," Miss Milton called after them as they set off down the road.

As soon as they were out of sight of the house, Hubert gave William a tentative punch, but received such a spirited one in return that he decided to keep relations on a friendly footing.

"I say, Bert," he said. "You're awfully like a boy I know called William Brown. I mean, you are just at first. I could see you weren't him all right when I looked at you prop'ly. But jus' at first you looked jus' like him. He's an awful boy. My mother won't let me play with him. I jolly well scored one off him to-day. I'm sellin' some mice, an' he wants one, an' I won't sell him one, an' he's as mad as mad." Hubert sniggered. "I say, I've got a jolly good idea." They were passing William's house and William was for hurrying past it with averted face, but Hubert stopped. "Let's play a trick on him. You go in an' go round to the back an smash the window in the tool shed. You're sure to find a ball or a stick or something lyin' about to do it with, an' you look enough like him for anyone who sees you to think you are him. An' I heard his father sayin' that the nex' time he broke that window he wouldn't have any pocket money for a month. It's a jolly good trick, isn't it? Go on. Do it quick an' then come out. There's no one about. I'll wait for you here. Go on. . . ."

William crept round the back of the house, watched by the sniggering Hubert. Then, out of sight, he entered the back door, slipped upstairs, changed into one of his ordinary suits, brushed his hair into its ordinary position, and came out of the front door with his usual sturdy tread, whistling, his hands in his pockets. Hubert, still crouching behind the hedge, anxiously watching the path that led to the back of the house, did not see him till he was almost upon him. Then he paled with horror.

"Hello, Hubert," said William in a tone of well-simulated surprise. "What are you doing here?"

Hubert blinked, gasped, and looked wildly at the path down which he had seen Bert disappear.

"I—I say!" he stammered. "There—there's a boy in your back garden. I—I was jus' takin' him for a walk, an'—an' he ran away from me down into your back garden. I—I told him not to, but he would. . . . I hope he's not doin' any damage."

"I'll go 'n' have a look for him," offered William cheerfully, and set off down the path where he had gone only a few minutes ago in the character of Bert.

He returned almost immediately.

"There's no one there," he said. "Who did you say it was?"

"He *must* be there," said Hubert desperately. "He only went round a minute ago. P'raps he's hidin' or somethin'. . . . He's a country holiday boy called Bert," he explained. "He'd gone to tea to Miss Milton's an' I—I was jus' takin' him a nice quiet walk down the road when he suddenly ran in at your gate and down that path. I called out, 'Come back!' but he went on. I say," as anxiety conquered his usual discretion, "do you mind if I come round an' look for him?"

"No," said William pleasantly. "Come on an' have a look."

"I don't know why he went round to your back garden," said Hubert again. "I—I kept tellin' him not to."

He peered nervously into the tool shed and the summer-house, followed by the grinning William.

"He—he can't have gone anywhere else, can he?" he said distractedly. "I—I don't know what I'm goin' to do if I don't find him."

"He might have got through the hedge into the field," said William helpfully, "but if he had done we'd see him in the field, an' he's not there. Of course," he went on with rising cheerfulness, "he might've fallen into the rain tub an' got drowned."

Hubert's pale face turned green.

"W-w-w-will I get hung for murder if he is?" he said.

"Oh, no," William reassured him. "They'd prob'ly let you off with jus' keepin' you in prison for life."

Hubert opened his mouth, and William saw that in another moment his howls would rend the air and bring out the occupants of all the houses near. He hastily peeped into the rain tub.

"No, it's all right," he said. "He's not there."

A slight expression of relief flickered over Hubert's face, then departed, leaving it pallid with anxiety.

"But what'm I goin' to do?" he demanded. "I can't go back to Miss Milton's without him. . . . And I can't jus' go home 'cause she'll ring up my mother an' there'll be an awful fuss. They'll say I oughtn't to have let him go, but—but he jus' ran round the side of your house quick as quick before I could stop him."

"Yes, there'll be a fuss all right," agreed William. "That cow in the field may've et him. Some cows do, you know. You can never tell with cows. They go on for years an' years an' years eatin' grass, an' then, quite sud'n'ly, they eat a person an' then they won't do it again for ten years or so——"

But Hubert wasn't listening to him. A sudden wild gleam of hope had come into his eye.

"I say, William," he said eagerly. "You *will* help me, won't you? I've got an idea. This boy was a bit like you. Jus' a bit. If you can sort of cross your eyes an'—an' hang your mouth open a bit an' walk sort of doubled up, they might think it was him. I bet Miss Milton's jolly short-sighted. People like her always are."

"But what about clothes?" said William. "Had he a suit like this on?"

Hubert's face fell.

"No, he hadn't, but"—it lit up again—"you could put on your rain coat, an' I could say that it looked like rain, so I called at the farm for your rain coat, an' she won't notice you've not got the same things underneath."

William considered, and a light beamed suddenly in his eye, too. At first he had meant merely to give Hubert a fright, in order to pay him out for his mean trick in the matter of the tool-house window. But now it occurred to him that more might be made of the situation than that.

"All right," he said. "I will if you'll sell me one of your piebald mice."

Hubert hesitated. He had widely advertised his refusal to sell the mouse to William, and he would lose considerable face if he did so, but the crisis was an urgent one, so with a sigh he agreed.

"Very well," he said.

William put his hand in his pocket and drew out his shilling.

"Here's the money," he said. "You can go an' fetch it now, an' then I'll put on the squint an' go with you to ole Miss Milton."

A few minutes later William was hiding his piebald mouse carefully in the wooden box, with holes bored in its surface for the purpose of ventilation, which had in its time housed many similar occupants. A layer of straw at the bottom served for bodily comfort—and a dog biscuit, lent, unwittingly, by Jumble, for sustenance. That done, William went indoors for his rain coat.

"Now, what d'you say this boy looked like?" he said in a business-like tone, as he came out, doing up the buttons.

"He had his hair brushed diff'rent," said Hubert, looking at him anxiously.

"Never mind that," said William, who didn't want to make himself look too much like the mysteriously vanished Bert in case it should arouse Hubert's suspicions. "A bit of hair doesn't make much diff'rence one way or another."

"Well, he had a sort of squint, same as I told you," went on Hubert.

William did a mild and tentative squint.

"What about that?" he said.

"Y—yes," said Hubert doubtfully. "That's a bit like it."

"Well, you can't expect me to turn right into him," said William, who was beginning to enjoy the situation. "If it's not right I won't bother to come. . . ."

"Yes, yes," said Hubert eagerly. "Do come. I di'n' mean that. It's jolly good."

"What else had he besides the squint?" said William.

"His mouth sort of kept open all the time."

"I bet I can do that all right," said William, opening

his mouth to about the size of a halfpenny marble.

"Y—yes," said Hubert. "I mean it's jolly good," he added hastily. "*Jolly* good. It's not *quite* like him, of course, but I bet she won't notice."

"Well, what d'you want me to do?" said William. "I've not got much time."

"Jus' come back to her with me," said Hubert, "an' say you've had a jolly nice walk with me an' that sort of thing, an' that it's time you went home now, an' then go off down the road as if you were goin' to go to Eastbrook Farm, an' I'll go the other way to my home, an' then if they say this Bert never got home she can't say it's my fault. I mean, I'll have brought him back from the walk all right."

"Oh, will you?" said William meaningly.

"I let you have the mouse," Hubert reminded him, with humble pleading in his voice.

"A' right," agreed William, as if reluctantly. "I'll come along."

"You needn't start doin' his face till you get there," said Hubert. "I don't want you to get it wore out before she sees it."

They walked down the road to Miss Milton's house. William preserved a strategic silence. Hubert kept saying—somewhat nervously—that he couldn't think why Bert had suddenly run round William's house like that, nor what had become of him.

"He jus' darted off. . . . I did all I could to stop him. . . . Corks! I hope nothin's happened to him. You—you *did* have a good look into the rain tub, didn't you?"

His face grew paler as they approached Miss Milton's.

"Go on," he said in a tense undertone, as they reached the gate. "Do 'em now."

**WILLIAM SQUINTED WILDLY AND OPENED HIS MOUTH
ALMOST TO THE SIZE OF A FOOTBALL, BUT IN VAIN . . .**

William did his modified squint and opened his mouth
slightly. The front door was open and Miss Milton was
telephoning in the hall.

She waved them in and went on with her telephoning.

"WILLIAM!" SAID MRS. BROWN.

She was evidently describing her guest to an acquaintance.

"He's just come in now," she said. "He looks better already. Less—*degraded*, if you know what I mean. He had a *dreadful* cast in his eye when first he came, but even this one day in the open air's improved it. Yes, I'd

love you to come and see him. Yes, come straight round.
You have a little boy of your own, haven't you? Could
he come, too? . . . Oh, he's out? . . . Yes, I quite
understand. . . . But *you'll* come, won't you? You must,
of course, be prepared for something very different from
your own child.''

She turned from the telephone to greet them.

"Well, dears . . ." she began brightly.

Hubert interrupted with a long, nervous account of
how they'd called at the farm for Bert's rain coat, and
then William, continuing his modified squint, said that it
was time he went home.

Miss Milton, however, insisted on hearing a detailed
account of their walk before he went.

"I suppose it opened a new world to you, didn't it, my
boy?" she said to William.

She was so relieved that the end of his visit was in sight
that she felt almost affectionate towards him.

Suddenly she looked out of the window.

"Oh, here's a lady who's kindly coming to see you,
Bert," she said. "You must just stay a few minutes
longer and speak to her. I'll just go and open the door."

They heard greetings in the hall, then the door was
thrown open and:

"This is Bert," said Miss Milton, pointing to him in a
proprietary fashion.

William squinted wildly and opened his mouth almost
to the size of a football, but in vain.

"*William!*" said Mrs. Brown.

"S'not William," protested Hubert vehemently.
"Honest, s'not William. He's *like* William, but he's not
William. . . . It's Bert."

"Of course it's William," said Mrs. Brown
indignantly.

Hubert persisted that it was not William, and Miss Milton supported him. Mrs. Brown said that a woman knew her own son after eleven years. William continued to squint and said nothing.

Then the real Bert, hot and breathless and dirty and gloriously happy, arrived. He'd had a wonderful afternoon at Marleigh, but on the way home had run into Mrs. Camp, who, discovering that he was wearing another boy's suit, had sent him round to retrieve his jersey. The altercation waxed fast and furious. Hubert and Miss Milton insisted more strongly than ever that Bert was not Bert, and that William was not William. Mrs. Brown said that she knew nothing about Bert. All she knew was that William was William. Everyone talked at once except William. William waited patiently for the hubbub to subside. He'd have to give an account of himself soon enough. No need to precipitate matters. Meantime, he was fixing his thoughts on the one bright spot in the whole situation. And the one bright spot in the whole situation was the piebald mouse. Bert or no Bert that, at any rate, was safely his. . . .

Chapter 4

Portrait of William

William was ambling dreamily along the road when the dreadful thing happened. It wasn't his fault. It wasn't the fault of the driver of the car. It wasn't really Jumble's fault, because he'd just seen a rat on the bank on the opposite side of the road, and he naturally couldn't be expected to think of two things at once. Anyway, he'd started off across the road like an arrow from a bow before William realised what he was doing. There was a loud screech from the car brakes, and a still louder screech from Jumble, the car stopped abruptly, and a girl leapt out from it, pale and dismayed.

"Oh, dear!" she said. "I *do* hope he's not hurt."

William was already lifting up the indignant Jumble and examining him anxiously.

"I *am* so sorry," said the girl.

"It wasn't your fault," conceded William, and added hastily: "It wasn't Jumble's fault, either. I bet it was that old rat's. When Jumble sees a rat, he jus' forgets everythin' else."

Jumble's cries of pain and anger still rent the air. William was wiping the blood from his leg with a handkerchief already so highly variegated with mud and ink that a little blood more or less made no difference.

"It's badly cut, I'm afraid," said the girl. "I don't

think anything's broken. Where's the nearest vet?''

"There's one over at Marleigh," said William.

"Well, let's take him straight there. You tell me the way. . . . Look. We'll make him comfy on this cushion. . . . Come on, Jumble. . . . Poor old chap!"

She lifted him on to the cushion so tenderly that he stopped whimpering and licked her hand.

"You sit with him behind," she went on to William. "We'll be there in no time."

They were at the vet's in less than five minutes. She praised and petted Jumble as the vet examined him. "Poor old Jumble . . . good boy . . ." and Jumble wagged his tail at her feebly.

The leg was washed, dressed and bandaged, the girl paid the bill, and William carried Jumble out to the waiting car.

"I just must go home first," said the girl, "then I'll take you and Jumble home."

William's heart was a-fire with gratitude. He remembered other motorists who had almost run over Jumble, and who had shown as much indignation and resentment as if it had been Jumble who'd nearly run over them. This girl, though she had actually run over him, had said not a word of blame. She had taken him to the vet's, paid the bill, and was now going to take them home. She looked about Ethel's age but was, William considered, superior to Ethel in every way. She had a worried look, too, that, William felt, wasn't altogether due to Jumble's accident.

"It's *jolly* decent of you," he said for the thousandth time, as he sat by Jumble, trying to stop him biting off his bandage.

They went right through Hadley and drew up at a fair-sized house on the other side of it.

"Stay here," said the girl. "I'll be as quick as I can."

She went in at the front door and closed it behind her. Almost immediately a man came out of the side door and said shortly to William:

"Oh, there you are! You've been long enough, haven't you? Come on."

William stared at him in amazement.

"Come on," ordered the man again irritably.

William looked down at Jumble, who was now fast asleep on the cushion, then, instinctively obeying the note of command in the man's voice, got out of the car and followed him indoors to a small sitting-room.

"Sit down there," said the man, pointing to a chair.

William sat down.

The man took a sketching block from the table and, standing in front of him, began to draw. His frowning gaze went from William to the sketching block, from the sketching block to William, from William to the sketching block. . . . When William fidgeted, he snapped, "Keep still, can't you?" so impatiently that William kept still. Once William remonstrated, "I say, I don't want to be drawn," but all the man replied was, "And I can tell you, I don't want to draw you," but he went on drawing all the same. After what seemed like several hours, the girl came into the room again. She looked more worried than ever.

"I can't find him anywhere," she said to the man.

"He's here," said the man, pointing to William.

"Oh, that's not him," said the girl.

"Good Lord!" said the man. "Do you mean to say I've been wasting all this time?" He looked at William. "Why on *earth* didn't you tell me?"

"I told you I didn't want to be drawn," said William

resentfully. "It's jolly well been wastin' my time as much as yours."

The man grinned and, for the first time, looked quite pleasant.

"I suppose it has," he agreed.

The girl was looking at the sketch.

"It's awfully like him," she said.

"Like Freddie?"

"No. Like him. Like William."

"Unfortunately it's Freddie we want," said the man, then, as if with sudden inspiration, went on: "Has this great aunt or whoever she is ever seen him?"

"No, I don't think she has. No, I'm sure she hasn't. She's lived in America for the last twenty years."

"And didn't you say she was old? Really old?"

"Yes, she's round about eighty."

He slapped his leg excitedly. "That's all right, then," he said. "She's far too old ever to travel to England. You shan't waste any more energy hunting for the little devil. This shall be Freddie." He wrote the name beneath the sketch: "F-R-E-D-D-I-E. Now all you have to do is to pack it up and send it to her."

"B—but——" protested the girl.

"No buts," he said firmly. "It's all settled. Let's get it packed up and I'll post it now."

"We'd better explain to William," said the girl.

"All right," said the man. "We'll explain to William. You start."

"Well," said the girl, "this gentleman—he's called Mr. Faversham—met Freddie's great-aunt in America."

"Freddie," added the man, "is a peculiarly objectionable specimen of the human boy, and this house is his domicile."

"Oh, but you've never met him," put in the girl.

"I know exactly what he's like, nevertheless," said the man. "Anyway, this lady—her name's Miss Bryce—has the misfortune to be mother's help in this establish-

"GOOD LORD!" SAID THE MAN. "DO YOU MEAN TO SAY
I'VE BEEN WASTING ALL THIS TIME?"

ment, and is bullied equally by the foul Freddie and his fouller mama."

"What *nonsense*!" dimpled Miss Bryce.

"Not nonsense at all," said the man. "Anyway, to continue the story, I met Freddie's great-aunt in

America, and she commissioned me to do a sketch of the obnoxious child and send it out to her. I made all arrangements for coming here and doing it to-day, but when I arrive, the obnoxious child has decamped—I gather that that's his idea of a joke—and can't be found anywhere. Miss Bryce takes the car to scour the

"I TOLD YOU I DIDN'T WANT TO BE DRAWN," SAID WILLIAM RESENTFULLY.

countryside for him, and comes back with a boy whom I naturally take to be the wanderer, and therefore sketch to the best of my ability."

"I was making a last search for him in the house and garden," explained Miss Bryce.

"Freddie's mother," went on the man, "is away from home, but she will pour out the vials of her wrath upon Miss Bryce if, on her return, she finds that a sketch of the boy was not sent out to the old lady. I have so many engagements that I couldn't come here again for several weeks and so—well, don't you see?—it would simplify the whole situation if this sketch could be sent out as that of Freddie."

"It doesn't seem quite *right*," expostulated Miss Bryce.

He smiled at her.

"Of course it's right. Anything's right that gets you out of a row with the old fiend."

"She's not a fiend," said Miss Bryce.

"Oh, yes, she is. You're scared stiff of her, anyway."

"She's—what you might call a martinet," conceded Miss Bryce.

"That's what I said," said Mr. Faversham. "Anyway, it's all right as long as this young man holds his tongue."

"You will, won't you, William?" said Miss Bryce. "It'll be all right about Freddie. His mother said that she didn't want him to know he was being sketched as it might make him self-conscious, so I can pretend that Mr. Faversham got him some time when he didn't know. You won't let me down, will you?"

"'Course not," promised William, who was still feeling a little bewildered. "But—I say, I'd better go 'n' see how Jumble is."

"Of course," said Miss Bryce. "I'll drive you home now."

"I'll wait for you," said Mr. Faversham.

"I thought you were in a hurry," said Miss Bryce.

"Not in such a hurry as all that," said Mr. Faversham.

*　　　*　　　*

William and the Outlaws were playing in the woods near Marleigh. It was several months since the episode of the portrait, and William had almost forgotten it. They had made a camp-fire and were sitting round it, smoking twigs to represent pipes and discussing the tribe of Mugfaces who were at present their deadliest foes. For Sir Gerald Markham, of Marleigh Manor, had engaged a new head keeper, by name Muggeridge (easily corrupted into Mugface), who not only displayed an energy and watchfulness that the Outlaws found highly disconcerting, but insisted on the other keepers displaying it, too. He was a blend of Hitler and Mussolini and Herod and Napoleon in his ruthless determination to stamp out his foes. And his foes were obviously the Outlaws, who ran wild in the woods, made fires, climbed trees, and even at times dared to raise their discordant and defiant war-cry. The old head keeper had been lazy and easy-going and content to chase them out of the woods occasionally in a perfunctory fashion. There was nothing perfunctory about Mr. Muggeridge's (or Chief Mugface's) pursuit of them. It was a thorough and highly organised proceedings. He sent his underlings this way and that to block exits, and himself, though a heavy man, plunged through the undergrowth with amazing speed. So far the Outlaws had managed to escape, but only last week Victor Jameson had been caught by him. Instead of being dismissed with a few resounding boxes on the ear, as had happened in the old head keeper's time, he had been dragged ignominiously to Marleigh Manor into the terrifying presence of Sir Gerald and forced to give his name and address. Thereupon, Sir Gerald, who was almost as much in awe of the new head keeper as if he had been a small boy himself, had written a fierce letter of complaint to Mr. Jameson, which had been delivered

in person by Mr. Muggeridge, still holding his victim by
the ear.

"Victor says he's still got bruises all down his arm
where Chief Mugface grabbed him," said Ginger.

"Huh!" ejaculated William grimly in his character of
Chief Hawk Eye. "Like to see him touch me, or one of
my braves. We'd *show* him all right."

"Yes, we'd *show* him," echoed the others, almost
convinced by William's manner that they actually would
show him.

"He daren't try it on with *us*," went on Chief Hawk
Eye. "He's jolly well scared of *us*, all right. He's seen
our bows an' arrers, for one thing. Yes, I bet he'd think
twice before he started on *us*. One arrer'd go right
through him."

The others looked rather doubtfully at the home-
made weapons that lay by them.

"Mine doesn't shoot very well," admitted Henry.

"Huh!" said William. "That doesn't matter. That
doesn't matter a bit. He's scared of 'em, all right. He's
so scared of 'em he jolly well wouldn't come near *us*. I'd
be jolly sorry for him if he did, too. *Jolly* sorry for him.
He'd jolly well get a bit more than what he bargained
for. Yes, those ole Mugfaces are scared as scared of us. I
bet if we met 'em now they'd jus' run off as quick as they
could. I bet——"

It was at this moment that Ginger suddenly said:
"He's comin'!" and the braves leapt to their feet,
leaving their weapons behind them, and fled with all
speed to the nearest exit from the wood. It wasn't till
they reached the road and stopped to take breath that
they realised William was not with them.

They waited for some time with growing anxiety and,
as he still did not appear, crept furtively into the wood

again to the spot that had been the scene of their interrupted pow-wow, but there was no sign of him.

Meantime, William was being dragged along by the hated Chief Mugface—a massive, grim-faced man with an iron grip that was proof against all William's wrigglings. William, unfortunately, had fallen headlong over a projecting tree root and, before he could get up, Chief Mugface had been upon him.

"You come along to Sir Gerald," he had growled, "and see what '*e*'s got to say to you. A-trespassin' and a-destroyin' of property. *An*' see what yer'll get from yer pa when he reads Sir Gerald's letter. . . ."

This last made William's blood run cold. He felt that his father's reaction to the letter would be highly unpleasant. In fact that very day his father, after receiving a wholly unjustified (as it seemed to William) complaint from a neighbour about William's taking a short cut through her garden and over her asparagus bed, had said grimly: "This is the last warning you get, my boy. One more complaint of any kind, and you're for it."

William continued to wriggle wildly, but in vain.

"You leave go of me," he muttered threateningly. "You jolly well leave go of me. I'll give you something you won't like if you don't leave go of me. You don't know who I am. I'm from Scotland Yard, I am. I'd come down jus' to catch a few trespassers an' suchlike for you. You'll get into trouble with Scotland Yard screwin' up my neck like this. . . . Leave go of me, I tell you. I say"—his voice became suddenly ingratiating—"I'll give you twopence if you'll leave go of me. . . . I'll give you more nex' week, too, if I get any. . . . *Stop* screwin' my neck up like that. . . . Leave go of me . . . I'm the head of a gang of gangsters, same as you see on the

"YOU JOLLY WELL LEAVE GO OF ME," MUTTERED WILLIAM
THREATENINGLY. "I'M FROM SCOTLAND YARD, I AM."

pictures. They'll shoot you if you don't let me go. . . .
Leave go of my neck. . . ."

Grim, silent, unmoved, Mr. Muggeridge led him out
of the wood, across a field, in at a gate, across a lawn,
into a house . . . into a pleasant spacious room where tea
was laid on a low table by the fire. Sir Gerald stood

by the fire, Lady Markham sat at the tea-table, the tea-pot in her hand, and an old lady wearing a hat and fur coat (obviously a caller) sat in an armchair between them.

Mr. Muggeridge pushed William, still muttering angrily and protesting in the same breath that he was a gangster chief and a Scotland Yard detective, into the middle of the room.

"Found another of them young rascals, Sir Gerald," he said, "a-trespassin' an' a-destroyin' of the woods."

Sir Gerald raised a monocle to his eye and inspected William through it.

"We've had to take a very firm line over this, my boy," he said. "The thing's become an intolerable nuisance. I'm going to write a strong note to your father, and Muggeridge, here, will take you home, and see that he gets it." He turned to the old lady. "These boys trespass in my woods so incessantly——"

But the old lady was gazing at William, a smile on her lips, a light of recognition in her eyes.

"Why, it's Freddie!" she said.

Sir Gerald dropped his monocle from his eye and Mr. Muggeridge his hand from William's neck. Lady Markham put down the teapot. They all looked at William. William scowled at them. "It's Freddie," went on the lady, laughing. "It's my great-nephew. I've never seen him before, but I had a portrait of him sent out to me in America a few months ago, and now I see him it's really a marvellous likeness. They live in Hadley, you know, but they're away just now. I thought that Freddie was away too, but evidently he isn't. . . ."

Sir Gerald's face had relaxed into a smile. Even Mr. Muggeridge's grim countenance wore a slightly constrained and apologetic air.

"In that case, of course," said Sir Gerald, "we'll have to let him off. You were quite right to bring him, Muggeridge, but—er—you can go now."

Muggeridge gave William a parting scowl and went from the room. Lady Markham smiled at William.

"Such a disagreeable man, isn't he? I've never liked him. Let's forget all about him. . . . Will you have some tea, dear?"

"Yes, have some tea, Freddie dear," said the old lady. "Then I'll take you home. How very strange to meet like this, isn't it?"

William agreed that it was. He made a hearty tea, answering in monosyllables when he was spoken to. At last the old lady rose.

"Now come along, Freddie dear," she said, "and I'll take you home."

William followed her out to a large car that was waiting at the door. Thinking that it would be a good plan to make his escape at this point, he said that he'd rather walk home, but the old lady said, "Nonsense!" and bundled him into the car. Host and hostess took genial farewells of him, calling him "Freddie the Poacher", and the car set off down the drive.

"Now, Freddie dear," said the old lady, "let's have a good chat. So glad I was there. Boys will be boys. I remember I used to do quite a lot of trespassing when I was your age. But I *was* surprised to see you, because I *quite* thought you were in Scotland."

"No," admitted William. "I'm not in Scotland."

His first impulse had been to tell the old lady the whole story and throw himself on her mercy, then it had struck him suddenly that the real story could get Miss Bryce into trouble, and she had been so kind to Jumble that he didn't want to do that. So he decided to play for time. He would answer all the old lady's questions in as non-committal a manner as possible, and escape as soon as the car stopped. If the real Freddie was in Scotland perhaps she'd never see him, and so the real story would never come out, and Miss Bryce wouldn't get into trouble. Anyway, with his glorious optimism, he hoped for the best.

"Of course," the old lady was saying, "my coming over to England was quite unexpected. I suddenly thought that if I didn't come now I might never come. I'm a very old woman, you see, aren't I?"

"Yes," agreed William absently. "Jolly old."

He was wondering whether he could possibly just jump out of the car and escape over the fields, but as it was going at about forty miles an hour he decided that he couldn't. If it stopped for petrol, however, he could easily do it.

"This car seems to me as if it wanted more petrol," he said with the air of an expert. "There's a garage jus' at the end of the road."

"Oh, no, dear," said the old lady. "I'm sure we've got enough petrol. Johnson's always very careful."

"I've heard of cars explodin' quite sudden with not havin' enough petrol in," said William darkly.

"I really think you're mistaken, dear," said the old lady.

Petrol was no use, evidently, but if it stopped for repairs he could still escape.

"Seems to me," he said after a slight pause, "there's somethin' wrong with this car. Feels as if a wheel was loose or sumpthin'. Funny sort of smell, too," he went on hastily, seeing that she was about to assure him that a wheel wasn't loose. "Smells to me as if somethin' was on fire. Cars *do* do that, you know. Catch fire quite sudden from nothin' at all. Don't you think you'd better stop an' have a look?"

The old lady smiled down at him. "What a nervous little soul you are!" she said. "No, it's *quite* all right, dear. Johnson says that the car's going better just now than it's ever done, so there's nothing at all for you to worry your little head about. . . . Now tell me, dear. Your people went to Scotland just before I arrived in England, didn't they?"

"Yes," agreed William, following the line of least resistance.

"I was sorry that I hadn't time to let them know I was coming to England, but I decided in such a hurry. And then, when I heard they'd gone to Scotland for the month, I didn't see any point in following them there. As I told your mother in my letter, I've taken a furnished house in Marleigh and there will be plenty of time for us to see each other when she comes back. It's really a cottage on Sir Gerald's estate. He's been so kind to me."

They turned a corner of the road just as Ginger, Douglas and Henry came across the fields from their fruitless search for him in the wood. They stared in amazement at the sight of William, driving in a Rolls-Royce, deep in obviously amicable converse with a strange old lady. He waved at them airily as he passed them.

"Friends of yours?" said the old lady vaguely. "Now tell me, Freddie dear, why didn't your parents take you with them to Scotland?" and while William was searching for an answer, went on: "Of course, I think it was very sensible of them. This motor-car touring is very bad for children. And so boring. Perhaps you wanted to be left at home?"

"Yes," agreed William, snatching eagerly at this explanation. "Yes, that was it. I wanted to be left at home. I said to them to leave me at home. I said I'd rather be left at home. I said leave me at home when you go away."

"But you aren't at home alone, surely dear?" said the old lady. "You're staying with neighbours, I suppose?"

"Yes, that's it," said William. "I'm staying with neighbours."

"Where do they live—these neighbours?"

And then William had a brilliant idea. The old lady would obviously offer to run him round to the neighbours. He'd give his home address, the old lady would drop him at the gate of his own home and then go on, and the whole problem would be solved. If she wanted to see his hostess he'd say very firmly that she was out for the day. Beyond the day, of course, William never looked. . . .

"They live jus' near here," said William. "Jus' at the end of the next road."

"What's their name, dear?"

"Brown," said William, and despite his optimism his heart sank somewhat as he thus rashly and finally committed himself.

"Are they the parents of a school friend of yours? Is that why they're putting you up?"

"Yes," said William, plunging yet more inextricably into the morass. "William Brown's my friend."

"I see, dear. Yes, it's an excellent idea, but I think I've got an even better one. I'd like you to come and stay with me till your mother comes back from Scotland. I am sure that this Mrs. Brown will agree, aren't you?"

William's eyes were glassy with horror, his tongue dry.

"No—no, I don't think she will," he stammered.

"I—I'm sorry, but I can't come to stay with you. I—I've got measles," he blundered on desperately. "I mean, I'm in quandarine. William Brown's got measles . . . he's got 'em bad. So bad no one can see him. I'd give you measles if I came to stay with you."

But the old lady only smiled.

"Nonsense, dear boy," she said. "If William's got measles, they'll be only too glad for you to come to me, and I'm sure I'm not frightened of measles. . . ."

She had given directions to her chauffeur through a speaking-tube and the car drew up at William's home.

"This isn't the house," said William frantically. "I made a mistake. I—I'm not stayin' here. I'm stayin' somewhere else, an' I'd rather walk to it. It—it's right in the middle of a sort of bog in a wood where the car couldn't get to it, an' I can easy walk from here."

But the lady only laughed gaily.

"Now don't start playing tricks on *me*, you little rascal! You stay in the car, and I'll just go in and ask this Mrs. Brown if I may kidnap you."

"She's out," said William hoarsely. "She's gone away for a week."

"But I can see someone at the window," said the old lady. "Isn't that she?"

"Yes," admitted William, "but it's no good askin' her anythin'. She's deaf an' dumb."

"Oh, well, I can talk on my fingers," said the old lady. "It'll be rather nice to have another opportunity of doing it. You stay here, Freddie. I'd rather talk to her alone."

William watched with the calm of despair while she went to the front door and was admitted by the house-maid. Through the window he saw her shaking hands with his mother in the drawing-room. Then he climbed from the car, entered the house stealthily, and crept up to his bedroom. He had a vague idea of barricading himself there and holding out against the world for several days. He had some humbugs and a packet of ants' eggs. . . .

Meantime the old lady was advancing upon Mrs. Brown with a pleasant smile.

"Forgive me for bursting in on you like this, Mrs. Brown, but I'm an aunt of Mrs. Shoreham's over at Hadley."

"Yes?" said Mrs. Brown, feeling slightly bewildered. She'd never heard of Mrs. Shoreham over at Hadley.

"I've come to beg a favour of you," went on the old lady.

"Yes?" said Mrs. Brown again.

"I want you to lend me Freddie."

Mrs. Brown stared at her in amazement.

"I beg your pardon," she said.

"Freddie. I happened to meet him this afternoon at Sir Gerald Markham's. I've taken such a fancy to him."

"I'm afraid I don't quite understand," said Mrs. Brown faintly.

"Of course you don't," smiled the old lady. "I rush in on you like this and blurt it all out. . . . I know, of course, that you feel responsible to his mother, but I've got a nice little furnished house at Marleigh, and a good maid, and really, he'd be very well cared for. After all, I am his great-aunt."

Mrs. Brown had turned pale.

"Really, Mrs——?"

"Shoreham."

"Shoreham," said Mrs. Brown. "I haven't the faintest idea what you're talking about."

"I'm talking about Freddie," said the visitor

patiently. "Your little lodger."

"My little——"

Mrs. Brown looked round nervously and measured with her eye the distance between herself and the poker. She might need it if this woman got violent. She was obviously mentally deranged.

"Yes. Surely I'm right in saying that Freddie is staying with you while his people are in Scotland. After all, he told me so himself."

"I'm afraid there's some mistake," said Mrs. Brown, trying to speak in a soothing voice. "Perhaps you've come to the wrong address."

"Hardly," said Mrs. Shoreham, "considering that Freddie brought me here himself. He's outside in the car now. Really, Mrs. Brown, I can't help thinking that you're behaving in a very strange way. The child would hardly have made up the story."

"In the car, did you say?" said Mrs. Brown, going to the window. Mrs. Shoreham joined her and they gazed at the car—empty except for the chauffeur—that stood at the gate.

"He *was* there," said Mrs. Shoreham, slightly taken aback. "Perhaps he's hiding. Let's go and see."

They went into the hall. William was just coming downstairs. He had decided that his room was too accessible and that it would be better to make for the open country. He stood there, petrified, glaring at them. Retreat was impossible.

"Oh, William," said Mrs. Brown, "do you know anything about a boy called Freddie? This lady's looking for him. She thinks he's staying with someone in the neighbourhood."

"But that *is* Freddie," cried Mrs. Shoreham.

William turned to her.

"NO, I'M NOT," SAID WILLIAM DESPERATELY. "I'M *LIKE*
A BOY CALLED FREDDIE."

"No, I'm not," he said desperately. "I'm *like* a boy
called Freddie, I know. Lots of people think I'm him. I
saw him get out of the car just now and go off down the
road. I know I'm jolly like him."

"Nonsense!" said the old lady. "You *are* him. I

couldn't possibly be mistaken."

Mrs. Brown sighed.

"Now, William," she said, "come down and tell us what tricks you've been up to."

It was while William was in the middle of a wholly unintelligible "explanation" that the other car drew up, and out of it came—Miss Bryce and the painter. But she wasn't Miss Bryce any longer. She'd left her employer and Freddie, and married the painter, and they were now on a honeymoon tour. She looked radiant and happy and prettier than ever.

"We were just passing through," she explained, "and suddenly we thought we'd call and see William, because it all began with William and the portrait."

"*What* portrait?" said Mrs. Brown despairingly. "William, *do* explain."

But William was tired of explaining. The crisis was obviously over, and the whole situation bored him. He was sick of Freddie and the old lady and people asking him questions. He was glad to see the former Miss Bryce again, but sorry that the painter had married her as he'd have liked to marry her himself.

"*He* can explain," he said, indicating the painter, then, to the former Miss Bryce: "Come and have a look at Jumble. I bet he's not forgot you."

Chapter 5

William the Dog Trainer

"Most of it was jolly good," said William judicially. "There was one soppy one all about people falling in love an' suchlike that made me feel sick, but it didn't last long, then there was a jolly excitin' one all about people fightin' from aeroplanes and shells burstin' an' things. My aunt said it made her head ache, but she once said my whistlin' made her head ache, so she mus' have a jolly funny head. The one I liked best was one about sheep-dogs. Gosh, it was fine."

They were sitting in Ginger's back garden—William and Ginger in the wheelbarrow, the other two on the grass. In the middle was a small heap of apples to which they helped themselves at frequent intervals. Ginger's mother had gone through her apple-storing cupboard, picked out those that were "beginning to go" and handed them to the Outlaws for the completion of the process. A fire of dead leaves burnt at the end of the garden. They had already investigated this (blackening most of the exposed portions of their persons in the process), and had finally been driven away by the gardener. So they now rested from their labours, reclining at their ease, munching their apples and listening to William's account of the "pictures", to which a visiting aunt had taken him yesterday—the last day of her visit.

"We had tea in Hadley after the pictures," continued William indistinctly through a mouthful of apple.

"What did you have for tea?" asked Ginger.

"She wasn't too good over tea. She said those doughnuts with cream in 'd make me sick, an' she only let me have two of them, an' only three of those coloured things with bits of coconut on. Kept sayin' I'd be sick. I was more like bein' sick with starvation with the bit she let me eat."

"Did she give you the half-crown?" said Ginger anxiously.

"Yes," nodded William reassuringly. "I got that all right. I washed extra clean this mornin' an' carried her suitcase downstairs while she was havin' breakfast. I had to take it back again 'cause it turned out she hadn't packed it yet, but anyway it showed I was tryin' to help, an' she couldn't get out of givin' me the half-crown. She made me promise to put it in my money-box, so I did all right, but I got it out again with a knife when she'd gone. I never promised not to get it out again. So now we can buy that box of fireworks for Guy Fawkes day."

"Good!" they said, much relieved, for, though they had counted on the half-crown, they had felt slightly apprehensive more than once during the visit, William's aunt having turned out to be definitely not a child-lover.

"What was the fightin' one about?" said Ginger, throwing a core at Douglas and hitting him neatly on the end of the nose. "Go on." He ducked just too late to avoid Douglas's retaliatory core. "Tell us about it."

"Well, it was jus' fightin'," said William, somewhat vaguely. "Bangs an' soldiers runnin' about an' people jumpin' off aeroplanes. There was a funny soldier, too, that kept fallin' into soup an' things. He made me laugh so much my aunt said she'd go out if I didn't stop. She's not got much sense of yumer. . . . But," he grew suddenly serious again, "it was this sheep-dog thing I liked best."

His eyes travelled speculatively to Jumble, who was investigating an imaginary rat-hole in a neighbouring border with that unflagging, if misdirected, energy that characterised most of his activities.

"There's nothin' int'restin' about a sheep-dog," said Douglas impatiently, taking another apple from the pile and digging his teeth into a bite of colossal proportions. "They jus' chase after sheep," he added in a muffled undertone.

"They jolly well don't," contradicted William heartily. "They jolly well do a lot more." Absently he considered the core of the apple he had just eaten, decided that it was edible, and crammed it into his mouth. "They act like yumans, same as you or I might, but a jolly sight cleverer. They get sheep from all over the place an' make 'em go through gates an' things an' herd 'em up together an'——" Again his eye wandered to Jumble, who was now sitting, panting happily, his nose covered with soil. He hadn't found a rat, but he was pretending that he had. "I bet Jumble'd make a jolly good sheep-dog."

"I bet he wouldn't," said Henry, choosing another apple and carefully scooping out a large bad part with a pencil which he took from his pocket for the purpose. "He's not the right sort of a dog. They have to be special sorts of dog."

"No, they've not," contradicted William. "You've only gotter train 'em right. They've just gotter be intelligent, same as Jumble is, that's all. It doesn't matter really what sort they are. I bet Jumble'd be better than most of 'em 'cause he's smaller an' could snap at 'em better. . . ."

The others were not interested in the potentialities of Jumble as a sheep-dog, or even in sheep-dogs in general.

"Well, tell us about the war picture," said Ginger, throwing a core up into the air and catching it neatly in his mouth. "You've told us nothin' about it yet, an' it's a jolly sight more int'restin' than sheep-dogs."

"I keep tellin' you it *wasn't* more int'restin'," said William irritably. "You won't let me tell you about it. They took 'em round all over the place—the dogs did the sheep, I mean—an' made 'em stand still, an' then made 'em go on, an' got 'em all inside a pen without anyone helpin' 'em at all. It was a sort of competition an' the best one got a prize. I bet Jumble'd get the prize easy if I trained him."

"Oh, do shut up about Jumble," said Ginger. "Go on, tell us more about that fighting one. What did they do?"

"I've *told* you about that," said William irritably. "There were a lot of bangs an' aeroplanes an' people runnin' an' killin' each other an' this funny man I told you about." Again his eyes wandered to Jumble. "Tell you what. I could hire him out to farmers when I've trained him. I bet I could make a jolly lot of money hiring him out to farmers."

"They've all got sheep-dogs," objected Douglas.

"Yes, but s'pose their dogs got ill or they wanted a bit of extra help or somethin', they would jus' send along for Jumble. I bet their dogs often get ill or want a bit of extra help or somethin'. I bet I'd make a jolly lot of money that way an' Jumble'd enjoy it. He likes chasin' things. I bet anyone that's as good a ratter as Jumble'd make a jolly fine sheep-dog."

"Bet you anythin' you like you couldn't make him a sheep-dog," said Ginger.

"All right," said William, his vague speculations now hardened into iron purpose. "You wait and see. You jolly well wait till I've got him trained, an' winnin' prizes all over the place, an' being hired out by farmers an' suchlike. You jolly well wait. . . ."

He walked home for lunch in a pleasant glow of exhilaration. Delectable pictures swam before his mental gaze. He saw Jumble rounding up hundreds of sheep without a single fault before an acclaiming multitude, saw his proud enemy Farmer Jenks approaching him humbly to ask for the loan of Jumble, as his own sheep-dog had hurt its foot. He had a lot of old scores to pay off as regards Farmer Jenks, and he decided not to make things easy for him. He'd charge him a bit more than the other farmers, too. . . .

"Well, I'll see," he'd say distantly. "I'm not sure I can let you have him. He's very booked up. . . ."

It wasn't easy to imagine Farmer Jenks's usually grim countenance humble and pleading, but he did his best.

"You'll have to wait your turn," he'd say, "an' anyway you couldn't have him to-day 'cause I'm taking him rattin'."

Yes, he thought that life would be quite enjoyable when Jumble was a famous sheep-dog.

Jumble, meantime, happily unaware of these far-reaching schemes for his future, trotted along the road beside him, occasionally leaving him to burrow in the ditch, worry an old boot, or scatter a heap of leaves by the roadside.

Later, fortified by a large lunch, William turned his attention to the practical side of the question. He had decided to carry out the training more or less in secret. It was clear that the Outlaws had little sympathy with the scheme. They were too short-sighted, of course, to realise its glorious possibilities. He wouldn't say anything more about it to them till he could confront them with the highly trained sheep-dog, winning prizes over the length and breadth of the country, and in constant demand among the local farmers.

"They won't have to make such a fuss about me trespassin' then," he thought, with satisfaction. "They'll have to let me go where I like."

He slipped into the larder, put a few currant scones into his pocket, in order to satisfy any pangs of hunger that might assail him during the afternoon, added a handful of nuts from a bowl in the dining-room (carefully rearranging the ones that were left in a not very successful attempt to make them look as many as before) and, whistling to Jumble, went down to the summer-house at the end of the garden, in order to concentrate undisturbed upon the problem. Jumble scampered along in front of him, still unaware of the storms of fate that were gathered around. In the summer-house he sat at William's feet and looked up at him questioningly. Not thus inactive in summer-houses was his master wont to spend the afternoon. . . .

William looked down at the squat, ungainly form affectionately. Good old Jumble! He was a jolly sight cleverer than any of those dogs in the film. He'd find it child's play being a sheep-dog. Pity that he'd wasted so much time teaching him to sit up and act dead. But, of course, he hadn't known then the glorious destiny that was in store for him. . . . Jumble, the world's prize sheep-dog.

But he must now consider the immediate future—the actual training of the prodigy. Sheep. It was no use trying to train a sheep-dog without sheep. He must first of all find some sheep for him to practise on. But where? His mind ran over the various farmers of the neighbourhood. Young Farmer Smith, who had recently taken Hurst Farm on the hill. . . .

William liked young Farmer Smith. He was unlike any other farmers of William's acquaintance. He didn't seem to regard William as his natural enemy. He joked with him and let him go over his farm and make friends with his animals. He let him help with haymaking, hay-carrying and threshing, too, and had told him carelessly that he could always go into his orchard and eat his fill, provided he didn't carry any away.

To William, Farmer Smith—in reality, an amiable, slightly indolent, easy-going young man—was a god-like hero, towering inestimably above all the other local inhabitants, whatever their imagined importance. He wouldn't charge Farmer Smith anything for the loan of Jumble. But he didn't want to train Jumble on Farmer Smith's sheep. He wanted to impress Farmer Smith. He wanted to burst upon Farmer Smith's delighted vision as the possessor of the world's champion sheep-dog (at his service whenever he wanted it). He didn't want Farmer Smith to watch the, perhaps, slow and laborious process by which this was accomplished, to see his mistakes (if he made any), to become familiar with every stage of the gradual transformation. No, he wanted to surprise, to stagger Farmer Smith by the glorious result. . . .

His mind, having begun on Farmer Smith, ran slowly over the other farmers of the district, and rested finally on his old enemy, Farmer Jenks. Yes, if he was going to practise on anyone's sheep (and he was), he'd practise on Farmer Jenks's. He didn't care what Farmer Jenks thought of him. He'd practise upon them, of course, in

Farmer Jenks's absence. Then, when he'd trained him, he'd try him on the other farmers, and finally reveal him, master of his craft, to his hero, Smith. . . .

Having thus settled matters, he started to his feet, called, "Hi, boy", and set off down the road, the unconscious champion frisking merrily about him.

He slowed his pace on reaching Jenks's farm. No use, of course, trying to do anything in sight of the farm and the lynx-eyed Jenks himself. He wouldn't do the sheep any *harm*, of course. . . . Well, it couldn't possibly do them any harm. It would be training them as well as Jumble. It would do them good. But one couldn't expect anyone as cantankerous as Farmer Jenks to understand that. . . . So he'd better go somewhere where Farmer Jenks couldn't see him. He walked slowly past the farm, trying to appear aimless and detached, in case Farmer Jenks should be anywhere about. Yes, there he was, crossing the farmyard and going towards the pigsties. Well, that was all right. If he was in his farmyard he couldn't be in his outlying fields as well. William decided to make for his outlying fields as quickly as possible and see if any contained sheep. Down the road, over a stile, across several fields, through a spinney (which, fortunately, would shield him from observation), and into the most outlying of Farmer Jenks's fields. Yes, fortune was on his side. Sheep. Masses of sheep. Browsing. Strolling about. Sleeping. Huddling together. . . . Ideal material for the training of Jumble. In order to make himself as like the men on the film as possible, William took off his coat, hung it on the hedge, and turned up his shirt sleeves.

He decided to regard the further corner of the field as his pen and to train Jumble to round up the whole field and concentrate them at that point. He assumed a resolute air, took from his pocket a whistle which he had brought with him for the purpose, and turned to the unconscious Jumble who was sitting scratching himself in a bored and desultory fashion till his master should decide to continue the walk.

"Hi, Jumble!" he called.

Jumble leapt up, wagging his tail to signify that he was ready and willing to continue the walk. But William was not continuing the walk. He was pointing to the sheep, sicking him on to them. "Go on, Jumble! At 'em, old boy! Fetch 'em out! Bring 'em round to that corner. At 'em, old boy! At 'em!"

Jumble hesitated. It had never occurred to him before to chase these large foolish creatures. Rats, rabbits, cats, of course, but not these big ponderous, slow-moving white things. Still, there was no doubt at all that that was what William wanted him to do. So he leapt among them, barking furiously. They fled in terror with loud, high-pitched bleatings. He pursued them in delight. It was marvellous. He'd never known anything like it. . . .

In a few minutes the field was full of scampering, bleating sheep. He pursued them round and round, lost to everything but the heady joy of the chase. William blew his whistle, called out his orders, but all in vain. Jumble's blood was up. He didn't even hear. Round and round. Here, there and everywhere. . . .

"No, Jumble," shouted William hoarsely. "Stop it, Jumble! That's not the way. Get 'em in that corner. In that corner over there." He pointed wildly. "Don't run 'em so quick. Get 'em all together."

Jumble ignored him, barking ecstatically, drunk with this discovery of his new power. Round and round. Here and there and everywhere. . . .

William decided to catch him and start again. He

hurled himself into the chase, making confusion more confounded. . . .

It was on this scene of wild disorder that Farmer Jenks appeared, drawn by the sound of barkings, bleatings, shoutings, from the field behind the spinney. He dealt swiftly with the situation, first sending a few well-aimed stones at Jumble, which convinced even that optimist that all was not well, then grabbing William by the neck and cuffing him soundly.

"You young devil!" he shouted. "You'll pay for this. Your pa will, too. Have you up in court I could, for this. An' I'm not sure I won't."

"But, listen," pleaded William wriggling ineffectively. "I wasn't doing any harm. Honest, I wasn't. I was only trainin' him. I was trainin' him to be a sheep-dog. I wasn't doing any harm at all."

At this moment, also attracted by the sounds of the pandemonium that had rent the air of the peaceful countryside, Farmer Smith appeared.

"Whatever's all this?" he said.

Farmer Jenks turned to him, his face still purple with rage.

"Caught the little devil in the act," he said, tightening his grasp upon William's neck. "Settin' his dog on to my sheep."

"I wasn't," said William desperately. "Honest, I wasn't. I tell you I was trainin' him. I was trainin' him to be a sheep-dog."

"Don't suppose the little beggar meant any harm," said Farmer Smith.

"Oh, didn't he?" said Farmer Jenks savagely. "Well, he's done it all right. Settin' his dog on to my sheep. I could bring him up before the justices for it, I've just told him, an' I've half a mind to. One thing's sure. That dog of his'll have to be destroyed, an' his pa'll have to pay for the damage."

"Oh, come!" said Farmer Smith.

"That's the rule, as you know well," insisted Farmer Jenks, "when dogs is found worritin' sheep, an' I seed this one doin' it with my own eyes. Dog destroyed an' damages paid for. Look at 'em yourself."

Farmer Smith looked at the sheep. They lay huddled together, panting and exhausted.

"Yes," he said to William. "I'm afraid you've done for yourself this time, young man."

"All right," said William, realising that it was useless to excuse himself further. "But you needn't tell my father. I'll pay for it all right. I'll bring you my pocket money every week till it's paid for. An' I won't let Jumble do it again. Honest, it wasn't his fault. I told him to. I was trainin' him. I——"

"Five pounds damage," said Farmer Jenks grimly, "an' the dog destroyed."

"Five——" Horror for a moment deprived William of the power of speech. "Five—— *Gosh!* Well, I'll pay it," he protested. "There's no need for you to go botherin' my father. I'll pay it, all right. I get twopence a week an' I'll go on bringin' it you till I've paid it." Farmer Jenks was obviously not impressed by this offer. "I'll go on bringin' it all the rest of my life," went on William wildly. "Look here, I'll do that if you won't go botherin' my father. I'll go on bringin' you my pocket money all the rest of my life. An' I won't let Jumble *look* at a sheep again. It wasn't his fault."

Jumble stood near, wagging his tail uncertainly, as if to add his entreaty to William's.

"I've had enough of this nonsense," said Farmer Jenks, tightening his iron grip on William's neck.

"CAUGHT THE LITTLE DEVIL IN THE ACT," SAID FARMER
JENKS. "SETTIN' HIS DOG ON TO MY SHEEP."

"Come on to your pa."

As he spoke he propelled him firmly towards the road.

Jumble followed, bewildered and chastened. He
didn't understand what was happening, but was quite
sure that it was something unpleasant.

By the time Farmer Jenks reached William's home,
his rage had so far abated as to make him assess the
damage done at the slightly lower figure of three pounds,

"DON'T SUPPOSE THE LITTLE BEGGAR MEANT ANY HARM,"
SAID FARMER SMITH.

but his insistence on the immediate destruction of Jumble, and his threat of "goin' to lor" if his demands were not immediately complied with were as determined as ever.

Mr. Brown dealt summarily with William, then rang up his solicitor, who advised him to pay the damage at the sum assessed.

"It's not unreasonable for a proved case of sheep

worrying. Magistrates round here wouldn't give anyone the benefit of the doubt, and there doesn't seem to be much doubt in this case. And I'm afraid the dog will have to go.''

"The dog!" exploded Mr. Brown savagely. "I should think the dog will go! That's the first thing I'll see to."

When William heard sentence of doom pronounced on Jumble, at first he could hardly believe it. He had looked on Farmer Jenks's threat as belonging to the "I'll break every bone in your body" class—not as one that would actually, and in cold blood, be fulfilled.

"He hasn't done anythin'," he protested passionately, "but do what he was told. I told him to chase those sheep 'cause I wanted to train him to be a sheep-dog. I keep tellin' you. He only did what he was *told*. Well, you don't murder a *person* for bein' obedient, so why should you murder a dog."

"It's no use arguing, William," said Mr. Brown sternly. "The dog must be destroyed at once. You've caused us enough trouble and expense over this, and the least you can do is to take your punishment quietly and not make a fuss."

"I wouldn't mind my punishment," said William, almost in tears. 'P'raps I *did* do somethin' wrong settin' him on to mischief, though, honest, I didn't mean to, but he only did what he was told. He didn't do anythin' wrong at all. He was only obedient same as you're always wantin' me to be. It would be a jolly sight fairer to have *me* destroyed. Why don't you have *me* destroyed. Why——?''

But at the look in his father's eyes—a look that boded, if not actual destruction, something not very far off, he stopped and, sacrificing valour to discretion, went abruptly from the room.

He continued his plaint to his mother, but even she was unexpectedly firm.

"It's no use, William," she said. "He'll have to go. Your father's definitely given his word to Jenks that he'll have him destroyed. There's no way out at all. It's your own fault."

"Well, what I say is," persisted William, "if everyone that's obedient's got to be destroyed, there'd only be the bad people left in the world, an' it doesn't seem fair to me."

"I can't help how it seems to you, William," said Mrs. Brown. "The fact remains that the dog must go. Jenks will bring an action for damages if he doesn't. He was very nasty indeed about it, and your father definitely *promised* that he'd have him destroyed. The vet's coming to do it first thing to-morrow morning."

It was a long and unexpectedly sad evening for the Browns. They had always protested that they disliked "that wretched dog", and would welcome any valid reason for getting rid of it. But now that William's old-established friend was on the point of vanishing from their midst, they felt strangely depressed. However, there was nothing to be done but to see that Mr. Brown's promise to the obnoxious Jenks was carried out.

It would be too much to say that William passed a sleepless night, but he certainly had—strange phenomenon for him—several wakeful periods, during which he wrestled with the problem before him as best he could. The first thing to do, he decided, was to take Jumble to the old barn and secrete him there. If his hiding-place was suspected he must find somewhere else for him. Ginger, Henry and Douglas would surely shelter him in turn—in cellars, lofts or outhouses. Jumble must live the life of a fugitive till the fuss had settled down. It wouldn't, of course, be much fun for him, but there was no alternative.

He slipped out early, fastened up Jumble in the old barn, came back and ate his breakfast in silence. The others also ate their breakfast in silence. Depression seemed to lie heavily over the whole family. Even Ethel refrained from ironic or gloating comment on the coming tragedy.

The vet arrived before they had finished breakfast. Jumble, of course, was nowhere to be found.

"Where's that dog, William?" said Mr. Brown sternly.

"Jumble?" said William with an air of surprise that was highly unconvincing. He left his breakfast, went into the garden, and called: "Jumble! Hi, boy! Jumble! . . . Wherever *is* he?"

Mr. Brown frowned impatiently and said:

"All right, go in and finish your breakfast."

William, glad of the respite, went indoors, but hung about inside the hall to hear what his father should say to the vet.

"Sorry you've had the bother of coming," he said. "The boy's evidently hidden the dog, but I'll send it round to you during the day." He turned to the gardener, who was an interested spectator of the scene, and who was known to cherish a deep-rooted hatred for Jumble. (Jumble could never resist digging up everything he saw him plant in case it might prove to be some new sort of bone.) "Go up to that old barn where he plays, and see if it's there." He turned to Mrs. Brown. "And will you ring up Ginger's people, dear, and the others, and tell them to keep a look out? . . . Well, I'll be going now."

It was then that a sudden realisation of the hopeless-

ness of his position assailed William. The grown-up
world was too strong for him. He had no chance against
it. He could find no hiding-place that would not eventu-
ally be discovered. Ranged against him were Farmer
Jenks, the gardener, his own family, the families of
Ginger, Douglas and Henry, all the adult population of
the village, intent upon the destruction of his beloved
friend. His optimism at long last failed him. There was
only one thing to be done, and it must be done without
delay. He and Jumble must leave this cruel place for
ever. The world was wide. They must run away and find,
if possible, some place where people were less
hard-hearted. . . .

* * *

Miss Wortleton had recently taken a large house on the
outskirts of Marleigh. Though a solitary spinster of
austere tastes, a large house was necessary to her
because of her large number of dogs. It wasn't that she
wanted a large number of dogs. It was that a large
number of dogs had been thrust upon her.

Miss Wortleton had been taught as a child to be kind
to animals, and the training had taken deep root in her
simple nature. It had grown with her growth, as a virtue
should, and now it dominated her whole life. She was so
kind that she could not bear to see an animal ill-treated
in any way, and being possessed, fortunately, of ample
means, whenever she saw an animal ill-treated, she at
once purchased it for whatever sum the owner demanded. Horses, of course, she sent away to Homes of Rest.
Dogs she took into her own home. Her own home was
full of dogs, for she was constantly seeing dogs ill-
treated. It was said that people would bring their dogs
from incredible distances in order to ill-treat them in

view of Miss Wortleton's windows, and sell them to her for five times their value. It was, in fact, because people in the north seemed so consistently unkind to their dogs, that Miss Wortleton had moved south, and taken a house in Marleigh. Even Miss Wortleton, however, was growing a little worried by the size of her canine household. It really left her no time for anything else. She had decided to get rid of some of her dogs, but, of course, she could not give them to just anyone. She must find a kind home, and Miss Wortleton's standards of kindness were very high.

The latest addition to her collection was Hector, a sheep-dog. Shortly before she left the north, she had come upon a farmer and his shepherd training two sheep-dogs. Both were making excellent progress, but one or two hidings were still due before perfection was reached. Miss Wortleton happened to witness one of these hidings and, after delivering her usual homily on Kindness to Animals, offered to buy the dog in question. The farmer was nothing loth. He had meant to keep one dog and sell the other for five pounds if he could get it. He asked Miss Wortleton for ten, and she paid him without demur.

Hector now entered that haven of kindness that was Miss Wortleton's home. He lived a life of pampered luxury, was taken for slow, gentle walks on a lead, fed upon chicken and liver, given soft cushions to sleep on. And, strangely enough, Hector did not appreciate it. He fretted and pined, refused the dainties offered him, and even on one or two occasions attempted flight. It was odd that, when ill-treated, Hector had seemed a healthy, happy dog, and now that he was surrounded by kindness on every side seemed sad and peevish. Miss Wortleton couldn't understand it. It was unsettling for the others.

And so she had decided to find Hector a kind home as soon as possible. In any case she really must do something to stem the tide of dogs that was flowing into her house, and she might as well start on Hector as on any of the others. But, of course, the home must reach her exacting standards of kindness. . . .

It was while she was sitting at her window, nursing a Griffon, who was suffering from a nervous breakdown, and pondering this problem, that she saw a boy and a dog coming down the road. They reached the crossroads just opposite her house, then the boy stood and looked up at the sign-post, as if wondering which road to take. The dog, wagging his tail, stood on his hind paws, putting his front paws against the boy's coat, and the boy laid his hand affectionately on the dog's head (William's treatment of Jumble was generally of the curt, manly variety, but to-day his feelings had been deeply stirred). The gesture of affection went straight to Miss Wortleton's heart. Anywhere that boy was, would be, she felt sure, a Kind Home. She could safely entrust any of her precious charges into his keeping. Hector would be quite happy with him. . . .

William was surprised to see a vague-looking elderly lady coming out of the garden gate opposite, and making her way to him across the road. He assumed his most aggressive expression. What was *she* goin' to make a fuss about? Couldn't be doin' her any harm jus' standin' in the road by her house. The whole world didn't belong to her, did it? But he saw, to his surprise, that she was smiling quite pleasantly.

"Er—do you like dogs, boy?" she began.

He glanced at her, puzzled and still on the defensive.

"'Course I do," he muttered ungraciously.

"Well then, dear," said Miss Wortleton, "I've got

quite a lot of dogs in my house over there. Perhaps you'd care to come over and see them."

Ordinarily, of course, William would have been delighted by this prospect, but he had at present weightier matters on his mind.

"I'm in a bit of a hurry jus' now," he said coldly. "I've a long way to go."

He turned away to continue his journey, and with his departure Miss Wortleton saw Hector's Kind Home vanishing into the distance.

An idea struck her.

"Perhaps you and your little dog would like some refreshment before your journey?" she suggested.

William's expression changed. He realised that he was hungry, and that the question of his next meal was an extremely problematic one.

"Thanks," he said gratefully.

He followed her across the road to her house.

Inside the house amazement descended on him. Dogs. All sorts of dogs. Dogs everywhere. In all the rooms. On all the chairs. On all the window seats. Two of them fighting on the stairs. And an idea struck him, in his turn. This lady evidently collected dogs, as he himself might collect caterpillars or cigarette cards, in unlimited quantities. One more or less would make little difference to her. If only he could persuade her to keep Jumble for a month or two till the fuss at home had died down. . . . No one would think of looking for him here and, if they did, they would hardly find him among this swarm of dogs. . . . He must approach the matter very carefully, of course. No use to tell her the true story. She'd ring up his parents and report to them if he did. Grown-ups always hung together. . . .

He looked around him.

It was a large room and, as far as he could see for dogs, well furnished. (The lady had turned a Peke off a chair, so that he could sit down.) Jumble would be quite happy here. He was already making friends with a Sealyham on the window seat. Yes, he must certainly manage to park Jumble here for a bit. Then, of course, he needn't run away. He was already tired of running away. . . .

The lady entered with a tray, on which was a glass of lemonade and a plate of currant buns. They were large new currant buns, and William's mouth watered. Gosh, he hadn't realised how hungry he was. For the next few minutes he was lost to everything but the deliciousness of the buns. When he had disposed of the last crumbs he looked round for the lady in order to offer Jumble to her as a (temporary) member of her household.

She was just coming in with a brownish, dejected-looking dog.

"This is a dog I particularly want you to meet, dear," she said. "His name's Hector. I think you'll like him so much."

Miss Wortleton had decided now at all costs to start the long-overdue process of reducing her canine retinue by presenting the disconsolate Hector to this kind boy. Hector looked up at William and brightened. Here was a boy. One of the species he had known in happier days who ran and jumped and shouted and threw sticks and stones. He put his front paws on William's knee, and gazed into his face, as if imploring William to take him away from this horrible place of boiled chicken and soft cushions and gentle constitutionals on leads. William put up a hand and stroked the silky brown head. His heart warmed to him.

"What sort of a dog is it?" he said for, despite his recent adventure, he knew very little about sheep-dogs.

HECTOR PUT HIS FRONT PAWS ON WILLIAM'S KNEE, AND
GAZED INTO HIS FACE.

"Well, dear," said Miss Wortleton, who was equally
ignorant, "it's just a—brown dog. It belonged to a
farmer who ill-treated it shamefully. I feel sure that you
would never ill-treat a dog, and so I tell you what I'm

going to do. I'm going to make you a present of it."

For a moment William's soul was rapt up by ecstasy, then came down to earth with a bump. He was here to dispose of a dog, not to collect one.

"I'm sorry," he said, "but I can't do with another dog just now. I—I was goin' to ask you to keep mine for me for a bit."

Miss Wortleton shook her head firmly.

"I couldn't possibly, dear. I've really got more dogs than I know what to do with. I've made a definite resolve not to take in any more, except, of course, in a case of flagrant cruelty. But," patting Hector's head persuasively, "I'm sure you'd never regret giving a kind home to this dear creature. He's no trouble at all, I assure you."

William looked longingly at Hector, then hardened his heart.

"No," he said. "I'd like to, but I can't. You see——" He stopped, remembering again that it would be fatal to tell her the true state of things. "Well, anyway," he ended lamely, "I don't want another dog jus' now. . . . But Jumble wouldn't be any trouble if you'd just let him stay here a week or two. Jus' for a little holiday."

"No, dear boy," said Miss Wortleton, still more firmly. "I must draw the line somewhere, and I've decided to draw it here. Think how nice it would be for your dog to have a friend. . . . Oh, you've finished the buns, haven't you? Let me get you some more."

She took away the dish and brought it back filled with fresh buns. They seemed bigger and better even than before, and as William ate, a rosy haze of optimism began to envelop him. After all, why not? He might never get another opportunity like this again. It seemed wicked to refuse such a gift. Surely he could devise some plan to meet the situation. And suddenly, with the last currant, a plan flashed into his head. He could hide Jumble, as he'd meant to at first, and say that he'd exchanged him for Hector. They couldn't insist on Hector's being destroyed, as Hector had nothing to do with Farmer Jenks's sheep. Or could they? Still upheld by his mood of glorious optimism, William decided that they couldn't. And then, later, when everyone had forgotten about it, he could bring out Jumble again and have two dogs. Fortified by this prospect—not to mention the plateful of buns—William set off homeward with Hector on a lead (provided by Miss Wortleton) and Jumble following. Miss Wortleton stood at the gate to watch him out of sight, beaming and waving at him whenever he turned round. She felt heartened and encouraged. She'd found Hector a Kind Home. Now she must really start on the others. . . .

William still felt optimistic and excited. Two dogs. He'd never thought he'd be the proud possessor of two dogs. He revelled in the sensation. Two dogs of his very own. Two whole dogs. . . . They seemed to be getting on together excellently, too. He let Hector off the lead, and he and Jumble raced and gambolled down the road. He took them to a hayrick that he knew to be rat-infested, and though they couldn't catch any, they had a hilarious time hunting them. Hector was wild with delight. After the boredom of the past month it seemed too good to be true. He was prepared to follow William to the ends of the earth if necessary. But as he approached the village William's pace slowed. He stopped whistling. His step became less elastic. His optimism was gradually deserting him. *Would* it be all right? Would his parents swallow the yarn? And, if they did, would they allow him to keep in Jumble's place a dog about three times the size—

especially after paying all that money to Farmer Jenks as compensation? The nearer home he got, the more unlikely this seemed.

Suddenly he stopped and listened.

The sound of some distant confusion reached his ears. It had a familiar sound. Bleatings, barkings, shouting. Well, whatever it was, it couldn't be Jumble this time. Jumble was trotting innocently at his heels. He decided to investigate. The disturbance seemed to be at the point where the lands of Farmer Smith and Farmer Jenks met.

William hurried to it. Yes, there they were. . . . Farmer Jenks had been trying to round up a large herd of sheep for market with a young and imperfectly trained sheep-dog, and the result exceeded even Jumble's efforts. Some of the sheep were scattered on the high road, some in one field, some in another, a few were in Farmer Smith's orchard, others were vanishing off the landscape altogether.

When William appeared, Farmer Jenks had just tied up his dog as worse than useless, and he, Smith, and two labourers (who had come to help) stood mopping their brows and gazing helplessly around them.

William's spirits rose. This was going to be worth watching. But bitter experience had taught him a lesson, and he took Miss Wortleton's lead from his pocket to secure Jumble. He wasn't going to have poor old Jumble blamed for this too. Then he looked round for Hector. He'd better hold him as well, or. . . . He stared open-mouthed. Like a flash of lightning Hector had streaked off into the thick of the confusion. He was greeted by a volley of oaths from Farmer Jenks, but Smith, who recognised an expert when he saw one, gave orders in the quick, sharp tone to which Hector was accustomed. Not that Hector needed orders. Hector had summed up the situation in one glance, and was delighted to be back at work after the long, weary boredom of the last months. The sheep, too, recognised an expert, and became calm and amenable. He hunted them quickly back out of the road, out of the orchard, out of the neighbouring field, rounded them up neatly in a corner and stood guard over them, panting with the unaccustomed exertion and blissfully happy.

William and Farmer Smith watched in silence. Even Farmer Jenks was devoid of his usual flow of speech. He stood, purple-faced, his mouth hanging open in amazement.

Then Farmer Smith spoke in a quiet undertone to William.

"Is that dog yours?"

"Yes," said William.

"Will you sell him?"

"Yes," said William again.

"Leave me to do the talking, then," said Farmer Smith. "I'll fix things up all right about Jumble."

Farmer Jenks was already making his way across the field to them. He scowled at William and grunted:

"That your dog?"

"Yes," said William.

"Dog like that's no use at all to you. Better let me have it. I—I'll give you a shilling or two. He's not worth much, of course. . . ."

Here Farmer Smith broke in.

"But, you see, the youngster must have a dog to replace Jumble here, who's got to be destroyed."

Farmer Jenks glared at Jumble, William and Farmer Smith, then cleared his throat and muttered:

"That's all right. You needn't destroy him. Wasn't his fault. Now about this other dog. . . ."

"Hector?" said Farmer Smith pleasantly. "Oh, he's just sold Hector to me. I've taken over that compensation payment as part of the price, too, so you and I can settle it together. I shall want definite proof of damage, of course."

The very air was lurid with Farmer Jenks's curses.

"You go off an' get that dog destroyed," he shouted at William. "It ought to have been done before now."

"Oh, no," said Farmer Smith. "You've said before these witnesses" (he pointed to the grinning labourers) "that it wasn't the dog's fault, and that he needn't have it destroyed. You can't go back on it. . . . I'll lend you Hector when you need him. Come on, William. Hi, Hector!"

They went off, leaving Farmer Jenks purple and spluttering with rage.

* * *

It was late that evening. William sat on the upturned wheelbarrow in the garden, whistling untunefully and watching Jumble worrying a bone that the cook had just thrown to him from the kitchen window. Everything had turned out successfully. Farmer Smith had accompanied him home and interviewed his parents. Secretly, and to their own surprise, they were relieved that Jumble need not, after all, be destroyed.

"You're sure that Jenks won't make any more trouble?" Mr. Brown had asked.

Farmer Smith had grinned.

"You leave him to me, sir. He's mostly bluff, is Jenks, an' he knows when he's beat. I'll settle this claim of his when I've gone into it. And he said the dog needn't be destroyed. . . . Don't you worry about Jenks. I can manage *him* all right."

Before he went he slipped a ten-shilling note into William's hand.

"That's for the dog," he said. "There may be a bit more coming. Depends on how I settle this compensation with old Jenks."

And so everything was amicably settled and, after a stern homily from his father (the chastening effect of which was counterbalanced by the thought of the ten-shilling note) William was, as it were, restored to ordinary life, his sheep-dog training episode forgiven and forgotten (except, of course, when it should be needed to swell the category of his misdeeds in any future trouble).

Jumble, who was going through an elaborate process of hunting and worrying the bone before burying it, threw it with his nose behind the tool shed, and pursued it with ferocious growls.

William rested his elbows on his knees, his chin on his hands, and went over in his mind the astounding incidents of the day. . . . Miss Wortleton . . . the house full of dogs . . . Hector's skilful display of sheep-herding. . . . Pity he couldn't have had longer to train Jumble. Pity he hadn't some sheep so that he could have kept Hector. . . . Though, of course, it was rather difficult to see how he could have done that in the circumstances.

It was at this point that Ethel came round the corner of the house. She had been spending the day with a friend, and knew nothing of the recent turn in events. She took it for granted that Jumble was now destroyed. William's attitude of meditating reverie—elbows on knees, hands on chin—she took to be one of intense dejection. She was not a hard-hearted girl, but she liked to turn circumstances to her own advantage when possible. She had heard her father tell William that his pocket money

"THAT'S ALL RIGHT, ETHEL," SAID WILLIAM. "I'LL FETCH
YOUR SHOES FOR YOU AND I CAN LEND YOU THE HALF-
CROWN."

would be confiscated for an indefinite period to help pay
the compensation, and she assumed that William would
be her willing slave, also for an indefinite period, at a
small remuneration.

"Oh, William," she said. "I'll give you a halfpenny if you'll go into the village and get my shoes from the cobbler's. A walk", she continued, "would do you good and help you to forget poor little Jumble."

William stared at her in surprise, then realised that she knew nothing of the stirring events of the last few hours.

"They'll be half a crown," she went on. "If you'll wait a minute I'll borrow it from Mother."

William rose, with an air of great dignity.

"That's all right, Ethel," he said kindly. "I'll fetch your shoes for you and I can lend you the half-crown." He flourished the ten-shilling note carelessly. "And you can keep the halfpenny. You may need it. . . . Hi, Jumble!"

Jumble came leaping out from behind the tool shed.

Immensely pleased with his gesture, and with the look of utter stupefaction on Ethel's face, still calling, "Hi, Jumble!" loudly, in order to emphasise his lawful possession of the ex-pariah, William swaggered out of the garden gate.

Chapter 6

William and the Vanishing Luck

Mrs. Brown glanced up with a smile from a letter she was reading at the breakfast-table.

"Aunt Lucy is coming to spend Christmas with us. Isn't that nice! I've asked her so often and she's never been able to come till now."

She looked round the table but saw no answering gleam of delight.

"Was there ever a family", groaned Robert, "with as many aunts as ours?"

"Well, dear, they're all very good to you," said Mrs. Brown mildly.

"Are they?" said Robert. "You're telling *me*!"

"Which is she?" asked William with interest.

Aunts, of course, varied. Some were better than others. . . . Some could be bent to circumstances, others bent circumstances to themselves. Some were generous, others were mean. If there had to be an aunt at Christmas (and there generally had) it was as well to know beforehand what sort it was going to be.

"She's Ethel's godmother," went on Mrs. Brown. "She's always been very good to Ethel, hasn't she, dear?"

"Er—yes," said Ethel, in a faraway, thoughtful voice.

Ethel's godmother. William remembered her. Kind, but touchy. Generous, but very easily offended. One kept out of her way as much as possible, and she gave one a handsome tip when she went.

"I know you wouldn't mind letting her have your bedroom, Ethel dear," went on Mrs. Brown, "and moving into the spare room. She says she can't sleep in a room facing north. You wouldn't mind, dear, would you?"

"Er—no," said Ethel, still in that faraway, thoughtful voice.

For Ethel was wrestling with a problem that had suddenly presented itself to her. Aunt Lucy usually sent her generous gifts of money for birthday and Christmas presents, but on her last birthday she had sent her a red and gold vase of indescribably hideous design. In an accompanying letter she said that the vase was of little intrinsic value, but had been given to her by her godmother, when she was Ethel's age, and so she gave it to Ethel, hoping that Ethel would treasure it as she had treasured it, and perhaps give it in later years to a goddaughter of her own. . . . Ethel, deeply disgusted, had put the vase on a shelf in her wardrobe, and finally given it as a birthday present to Dolly Clavis, as a retaliation for the hot-water bottle cover that Dolly had given her, and that she knew had been given to Dolly by her grandmother. And now Aunt Lucy was coming to stay with them for Christmas. She was even going to sleep in Ethel's room. She was one of those people who still retain a kind of proprietary interest in their presents, expecting to see them holding places of honour on every occasion for ever afterwards. She would look for it eagerly as soon as she arrived. If it weren't on the drawing-room mantelpiece, it should at any rate be on the mantelpiece in Ethel's bedroom. And it wasn't on either. It was at Dolly Clavis's, unless she, in return (as was more than likely), had disposed of it in some way. Ethel might, of course, have approached Dolly, but this, in the circumstances, was impossible. She and Dolly were passing through one of their periodic phases of not being on speaking terms (on this occasion because someone had told Dolly that Ethel had said that blue didn't suit her). Dolly, moreover, was spiteful and, in the present state of things, quite capable of giving her away to Aunt Lucy.

No. . . . Her eyes wandered to William, who, having consumed a large plateful of bacon and eggs, now sat wolfing bread and marmalade, as if, thought Ethel dispassionately, he hadn't seen food for months. She refrained, however, from her usual ironic comments on the manner and matter of his meal. As denizens of the underworld turn for help to professional criminals in time of crisis, so Ethel was turning to William. . . . William was hard up. Owing to a recent conflict with authority he had no money to buy Christmas presents. For sixpence, she knew, he'd do almost anything. . . . He was not, of course, particularly discreet, but she wasn't in a position to pick and choose. There were only three days before Christmas. She followed him into the garden after breakfast and approached him cautiously.

"Hello, William," she said.

She overdid the kindness of her voice and he glared at her suspiciously.

"What d'you want?" he said. "I'm not goin' upstairs for anythin'."

"Would you like to earn sixpence?" went on Ethel.

William's expression changed.

"Well, yes," he said. "I wouldn't mind earnin' sixpence. I've almost forgot what money looks like," he added bitterly.

"Well, listen . . ." said Ethel.

She told him the whole story.

He listened uncomprehendingly. He'd have come to the conclusion that grown-ups were mad, if he hadn't already come to it years ago. He understood, however, that Ethel wanted him to get the vase back from Dolly Clavis, and that Dolly Clavis was not to know why she wanted it back.

"You mustn't, in any circumstances, of course, steal it," she said virtuously, hoping nevertheless that he'd stick at nothing.

" 'Course I won't steal it," said William. "I don't say I mightn't—jus' sort of borrow it."

"That's nothing to do with me," said Ethel aloofly, "but if you can get it back just while Aunt Lucy is here, I'll give you sixpence."

"Will you give me threepence now?" bargained William.

Ethel considered.

"All right," she said at last.

William pocketed the threepence and set off for Mrs. Clavis's house. He walked with slow, purposeful step, his brows knit into a stern frown, planning his campaign. . . . He knocked loud and long at the door and was shown into the morning-room, where Mrs. Clavis was telephoning the butcher.

"Good morning, dear. . . . It was *much* too fat last time. . . . How's your mother? . . . I must have it in time for lunch. It's been late every time I've ordered it lately. . . . Sit down, dear . . . I don't know what the boy *does* on the way. He looks as if he went through the hedge several times. . . . No, I don't mean you, dear. . . . Well, if it doesn't get here till one o'clock, it's hardly in time for lunch, is it? . . . Would you like a biscuit or is it too soon after breakfast? . . . No, I'm speaking to someone at this end. . . . If it's not here by twelve I shall simply send it back."

She put down the receiver and turned her large, good-natured smile on William.

"People *are* so stupid, aren't they?" she said.

"It's not too soon after breakfast," said William hopefully.

"Oh, of course. . . ."

She went to the dining-room and returned with a tin of mixed biscuits.

"They're a bit musty, I'm afraid."

"Thanks awfully," said William gratefully. "I don't mind a bit of must."

He set to work with silent concentration, and she watched him with interest and a certain awe. Really, if one didn't know his parents personally, one would think he was starved. . . .

"Well, dear," she said at last, "I suppose you've brought a message from your mother about the Sale of Work. We're all getting very busy with it now, aren't we?"

William swallowed the last of the biscuits and brought his mind to bear on the matter in hand.

"Well, not exactly," he said, as if the question had been very near the truth. "Not *exactly* about the Sale of Work. I mean—well, d'you remember that vase Ethel gave Dolly for her birthday present? A red an' gold one?"

"Yes, dear," said Mrs. Clavis. "I do remember. I thought it such a very odd present to give her, and so did Dolly."

"She gave it her 'cause she thought she'd like it," said William emphatically. "She took a lot of trouble givin' it her 'cause she thought she'd like it. . . . Well, we've got a friend comin' over to-morrow who's sort of int'rested in vases. In red an' gold ones, that is. An' he—she—they want to have a look at this red an' gold vase 'cause—'cause they're int'rested in red an' gold vases."

"How very odd!" said Mrs. Clavis. "But, of course, they can see it. Tell your mother to bring them to tea. How many did you say?"

"Oh, they're too many to bring to tea," said William hastily. "I mean, there's ever so many of them. Well, I mean there's one or two. But they've got special instruments for studyin' vases an' they're much too big to take out to tea with them. They'll want to have this vase about a week to study it prop'ly." He suddenly remembered Mrs. Clavis's ineradicable interest in her neighbours' affairs, and added: "You won't see 'em in the village or anywhere. An' you won't see 'em if you come to our house either. They—they don't do anythin' but study vases. Red an' gold vases. They—they stay up in their rooms all day studyin' vases."

"I never heard anything so extraordinary," said Mrs. Clavis. "Never in all my life. I'm quite sure, my dear boy, that you've got hold of the story, whatever it is, quite wrong. You are a little apt to confuse things, you know, dear. I've often noticed it."

"Well," said William, playing for safety, "p'raps I've got it a bit wrong, but they did ask me to borrow that vase for a week while Aunt—I mean, they did want you to lend 'em that vase jus' for a bit."

"I'm not sure where it is," said Mrs. Clavis vaguely, "but I'll go and ask Dolly. She isn't up yet. She was at a dance last night."

She went out and William whiled away the time by finishing up the crumbs from the biscuit jar.

After a few minutes Mrs. Clavis returned. She threw a pained but resigned glance at the crumb-strewn carpet round William's feet, then said:

"Well, dear, I don't quite know what to say. It seems that Dolly gave it away as a prize at that whist drive we had while Ethel was away. I'd quite forgotten till she reminded me just now. She told me not to tell you, but I always think the truth's best, don't you? In any case it was a very odd present to give Dolly for a birthday present. . . ."

William was silent for a moment. This was an unexpected set-back. The sixpence wasn't going to be so easily won, after all. . . .

"It was a jolly good vase," he said at last. "She gave it to her 'cause she thought she was int'rested in vases. . . . Mos' people are int'rested in vases, an' Ethel nat'rally thought she was. Same as mos' people are. Who—who won it?"

"Let me see," said Mrs. Clavis. "I don't quite remember. I know that practically everyone revoked and hardly anyone added up their score right. Oh, yes. I remember now. It was Peggy Barlow. We thought she was very ungracious about the vase. It was", she veered round suddenly to William's point of view, "a very pretty vase and, I'm sure, quite valuable in its way. At any rate, there was no need to make fun of it, as Dolly distinctly saw her doing, though she said she was laughing at a joke she'd suddenly thought of and then forgotten. After all, a vase *is* a vase, and she was only the first by a few marks, so there was no need for her to put on airs."

"Oh," said William. "Well, thanks very much. . . ."

"You'd better not tell Ethel that Dolly gave the vase away," said Mrs. Clavis. "Young people are so touchy, aren't they? You mustn't tell an untruth, of course. Perhaps you'd better say we've mislaid it. And, as for these people coming here to study vases—well, dear, I'm *quite* sure you've got hold of the wrong tale. Mind you, I don't blame Dolly for giving it away, because I think it was a very odd present for Ethel to have given the poor girl on her birthday, but all the same—You in a hurry, dear? Well, I won't keep you. Give my love to your mother, and tell her I'm looking forward to the Sale of Work, will you? Good-bye, dear."

William hurried off towards the Barlows' house. His story had sounded less convincing than he had thought it would. He'd better think out something else for Peggy—something a little more subtle.

She was just coming out of her house as William reached the gate.

"Hello, William," she said distantly. William was not popular with any of Ethel's friends.

"Hello," said William in a nauseatingly effusive tone. He began to walk down the road with her. "It's a jolly nice morning, isn't it?" he went on conversationally.

"No, I don't think so," said Peggy coldly.

"No, it isn't, is it?" he agreed hastily. "I think it a jolly rotten mornin'. I say, Peggy, did you know I was int'rested in paintin' an' suchlike?"

"No, I didn't," said Peggy. "I didn't know you were interested in anything but making a nuisance of yourself."

William felt no particular resentment at this. It was the tone that Ethel and Robert and all their friends normally adopted to him, and he would have felt embarrassed by any other.

"Well, I am," he said. "I'm jolly int'rested in paintin'. I want to get hold of a red an' gold vase to paint. I want to draw it on paper an' then paint it. It's a red an' gold one I want particular. I—I wondered if you knew anyone what'd lend me one?"

He smiled complacently, pleased by the depth of cunning displayed by this manœuvre.

But Peggy merely said, "No, I don't," and walked on in silence.

William decided to be a little less subtle.

"Well, I called at Mrs. Clavis's to ask if she'd got one to lend me. Jus' for practice in drawin' and paintin'. I want to practise drawin' an' paintin', you see, an' someone what knows a lot about it told me that the best way to learn drawin' an' paintin' was to copy red an' gold vases. Well, I sort of thought Mrs. Clavis might have one, an' I called an' asked her, an' she said she hadn't, but she said that you'd got one what you got for a prize at their whist drive."

Peggy's air of nonchalance fell from her.

"That thing!" she said, in a voice that quivered with emotion. "*That* thing! What a neck giving *that* for a prize! I'd have been ashamed. Who wants a vase, anyway?"

"She says a vase is a vase," put in William mildly.

"Yes, it is, worse luck! You wouldn't have thought a box of chocolates would have ruined them, would you? Or even a box of cigarettes. She must have won it at houp-la, but how she'd got the neck to give it for a prize beats me. It was all I could do to be polite about it—if I was, and I'm not sure that I was. I'd a jolly good mind to give it back to Dolly on her birthday, just to show them what I thought of it, but it was my birthday the week after so I didn't like to risk it. But—well, the *neck* of it! A *vase*! There was I slaving all night trying to remember what had gone and all I got was a potty little *vase*!"

"And—er—what did you do with it?" said William, striving to preserve a note of detachment in his voice.

"*Do* with it? I stuck it on the spare-room mantelpiece along with all the other junk, and I jolly well hope she saw it there the next time she came to the house. That'd show her what I thought of the wretched thing."

"I'M JOLLY INT'RESTED IN PAINTIN'. I WANT TO GET HOLD OF A RED
AN' GOLD VASE TO PAINT."

William's eyes gleamed hopefully. At last the end of
his quest was in sight.

"Well," he said, "p'raps you'd kindly let me go 'n'
fetch it jus' to practise drawin' an' paintin', same as I
said."

"Oh, it's not there now," she said carelessly. "When Miss Jones came round last week asking if I'd got anything for her rummage stall at the Sale of Work I said she could have it and good riddance. And I jolly well hope Dolly Clavis sees it on the rummage stall. Well, no one's likely to *buy* it, so she will if she's there at all. And *that*'ll show her what people think of her. Hours of counting up what had gone and all for a potty vase that was given away with a pound of tea."

"I think it was a *good* vase," put in William.

"What do you know about it?" said Peggy crushingly.

"Nothin'," said William hastily. "Nothin', I only meant it *might*'ve been a good one. I mean, Aunt Lucy——"

"What's *she* got to do with it?"

"Oh, nothin', nothin'. Where does this Miss Jones live?"

"She lives in Hadley."

"P'raps I could go 'n' borrow it from her."

"No, you can't," said Peggy. "She's away and she's got all her rummage things locked up in her box-room, and the house is shut up, and she's not coming back till the morning of the sale. She told me so."

There was a malicious satisfaction in her tone. She was the sort of girl who is glad to put a spoke in anyone's wheel. William wanted the vase and so she was glad he couldn't have it. Again William wondered at the blindness that made men admire such creatures. But this was no moment to be pondering abstract problems. Miss Jones (whoever she was) wasn't coming back till the morning of the sale. Aunt Lucy, who was going to the sale, would see her precious vase in the centre of the rummage stall. She would be outraged. She would never give Ethel anything else. This fact weighed little with William. What did weigh with him was the fact that he wouldn't get the rest of his sixpence.

"In Hadley, did you say?" he said.

"Yes, the corner house in Elm Avenue, you know. But it's no good going there. She's away. But why must you have a vase? Why can't you draw leaves and things like other people? Anyway, I can't imagine *you* drawing anything. Anyone less——"

"Goodbye," said William, setting off briskly in the direction of Hadley.

He found Elm Avenue. He found the corner house. It appeared to be unoccupied. He wandered round it for some time and finally discovered that the window of a room upstairs—presumably a bedroom—was open, near to a convenient drainpipe. Drainpipes were William's speciality. Neighbours for miles round borrowed him when they'd forgotten their latch keys. No one seemed to be about. He scrambled up and opened the window cautiously. It didn't look like a box-room and he didn't see any rummage about but—Joy! There was the red and gold vase on the mantelpiece. He climbed into the room and put the vase carefully in his pocket, scrambled safely down the drainpipe again, and set off homeward. Ethel had gone out for lunch, so he couldn't claim his threepence at once. Thinking that his mother would be certain to disapprove of his method of reclaiming the vase, he said nothing to her of his adventures, but put the vase on the morning-room mantelpiece where Ethel would see it at once when she came home, and then went in to lunch.

"William, dear," said Mrs. Brown, as she gave him his third helping of jam tart, "I'm having some people to tea this afternoon. We don't want to be disturbed, so perhaps you'd go over to Ginger's?"

"Oh, yes," agreed William amicably. "I bet I jolly well don't want to see them any more than what they want to see me. . . . Can I eat up what's left over from tea?''

"It depends what's left over, dear. You can have any sandwiches that are left and one piece of each cake."

JOY! THERE WAS THE RED AND GOLD VASE ON THE MANTELPIECE.

William considered this offer in silence.

"What size of a piece?" he demanded at last and added, "I'll stay out till bedtime if you'll let me cut my own."

"No, William," said Mrs. Brown firmly. "You cut almost the whole cake the last time I let you do that. Anyway, there's no need for you to stay out till bedtime.

Come in for your tea at five o'clock as usual. I only don't want you about the house all afternoon."

"I don't want myself about either," said William. "Askin' me if I like school an' suchlike! I'll come in about half-past five, shall I? I bet they'll be goin' about then, won't they? . . . An' I bet they eat up all that cake with nuts on," he ended bitterly, "an' leave the seed cake. . . ."

Mrs. Brown's tea-party consisted chiefly of ladies who were on the committee of the Sale of Work, and the conversation turned chiefly on arrangements for the sale.

"Miss Jones is in charge of the household stall as usual," said Mrs. Monks, the Vicar's wife. "I suppose she'd like the corner by the door that she generally has. She says it's draughty but it catches people coming in. . . . I don't know whether anyone else would like it. It seems unfair for Miss Jones to have it year after year if anyone else would like it. Of course, as she says, it means a dreadful cold afterwards, but—well, you *do* catch people coming in. . . ." She looked at Mrs. Brown. "You did say she was coming to-day, didn't you, dear?"

"Yes," said Mrs. Brown, "and she's generally so punctual. I expect she'll be here soon. . . ."

But Miss Jones, generally so punctual, didn't arrive till they were well under way with the Fancy Stall. She was small and plump, and wore as a rule a placid, amiable expression, but to-day her expression was harassed and distraught. . . .

"Oh *dear!*" she said, as she sank down into an armchair. "I'm sorry but I simply can't think about the Sale of Work. . . . Yes, I'll have the corner by the door. . . . It'll probably give me pneumonia, but you catch people coming in, and it's all for the cause. . . . I'm in such trouble that I can't give my mind to anything. My Luck's gone. . . ."

"Your Luck, dear?" said Mrs. Monks.

"Yes. It's silly of me, of course, to call it my Luck, but I always have done ever since I can remember. It's a Crown Derby vase that used to belong to my grandfather and he left it to my mother and my mother left it to me. I've always been very fond of it and called it my Luck. When I was a girl I really used to believe that it was my Luck. . . . You know, that everything would go wrong with me if I lost it, and I can't help feeling a little the same about it now. I'm terribly distressed. I've notified the police, of course, and there's nothing else that one can do at present."

"But what's happened to it, Miss Jones?" asked Mrs. Brown.

"It's gone. *Stolen*. And nothing else has gone. That's the odd part of it. It's very queer, and it makes me very uneasy. However, I don't want to be selfish. I know we aren't here to discuss my troubles. . . . Yes, I'll have the corner near the door, but I must *insist* on a better screen than I had last year. There was a large hole and the wind just hurtled through. . . . I don't want to be superstitious, but I feel, with my Luck gone, that *anything* might happen. . . . It seems so odd for the thief just to have taken that and nothing else. It seems that there must be some *meaning* in it. . . . Yes, I agree that Teas should be one shilling. One barely covers expenses at ninepence. Some of them seem to eat so much more than is necessary. . . . After all, there was my jewel case in my bedroom, and one or two quite valuable old snuff boxes on the mantelpiece with the Luck, and it seems so odd that the thief should just have taken the Luck and nothing else. . . . Almost as if—as if he *knew* something. . . . I'm sorry to keep *harping* on it so. Let's go on discussing the Sale of Work."

After a somewhat perfunctory tribute of interest in the loss of Miss Jones's Luck (after all, as Mrs. Monks murmured to Mrs. Milton under cover of the general conversation, what *did* it matter in comparison with a cause like the Village Hall Heating, and in any case she disapproved of superstition, and had always thought there was something ostentatious about Crown Derby), they returned to the subject of the Sale of Work. ("Let's keep to the simple, old-fashioned title," said Mrs. Monks. "Fête, I always think, sounds so pretentious, and Bazaar so Eastern.")

After tea Mrs. Brown asked them if they'd like to see the contributions she had already had for her Fancy Stall.

"It's really quite a nice little collection," she said modestly. "I've put it out on the dining-room table in case you'd care to see it. Rather too many tray-cloths, of course, but then, that's always the trouble. . . ."

She led them down the passage, past the morning-room, to the dining-room. They stood round the dining-room table admiring the little pile of tray-cloths, embroidered mats, and knitted baby-wear (some of elephantine proportions) that lay there. All except Miss Jones. Miss Jones remained at the door of the morning-room paralysed by amazement, staring open-mouthed at the vase that stood on the mantelpiece. It *couldn't* be. It couldn't *possibly* be. . . . But it was. . . . It *was*. . . .

"Where's Miss Jones?" said Mrs. Brown, from the dining-room.

On an impulse Miss Jones darted into the morning-room. . . . Yes, it had that little chip on the base. . . . She'd have known it anywhere. . . . It was. . . . It *was*. . . .

"Miss Jones!" called Mrs. Monks.

Pale and breathless, Miss Jones rejoined the others in the dining-room.

"Isn't this a pretty tray-cloth?" said Miss Milton.

"I'd have known it anywhere," said Miss Jones hysterically.

She was very silent when they returned to the drawing-room to discuss the printing of tickets and posters. The others, however, were so deeply engrossed in the question that no one heard William return and come into the hall for an air-gun that he had left in the umbrella stand. He passed the open door of the morning-room and saw the vase on the mantelpiece, and it occurred to him suddenly that it was too public a position. His mother might see it and ask how it got there. The less his mother knew about the whole affair the better. He'd better keep it hidden till he'd handed it over to Ethel, and then it would be Ethel's responsibility, not his. He slipped into the morning-room, took it from the mantelpiece and went up to Ethel's bedroom. It would be all right there. No one would go in there till Ethel came home, so he couldn't be called to account for it. . . . He went quickly downstairs, took his air-gun from the stand, and returned to Ginger's.

Miss Jones sat dazed and silent in the drawing-room while printers' quotations and colours of posters ebbed and flowed about her unheeded. Why—*why*—why—had Mrs. Brown stolen her Luck? Wild theories swam through her mind. She'd beaten Mrs. Brown last month by two marks in the Women's Guild jam-making competition. They were both going in for the quilting competition next month. . . . *Could* it be that Mrs. Brown had deliberately taken her Luck in order not to be beaten by her again? Oh, no, it was impossible. Then why was her Luck on the morning-room mantelpiece of Mrs. Brown's house? She must get to the bottom of it.

She couldn't bear this uncertainty any longer. She rose jerkily to her feet.

"Mrs. Brown," she said in a voice that she tried to make ordinary, but that sounded squeaky and high-pitched, "I—I'm so much interested in Crown Derby vases. I'd be so glad if you'd kindly let me examine the one that's on your morning-room mantelpiece."

Mrs. Brown stared at her in amazement.

"There isn't a Crown Derby vase on the morning-room mantelpiece, Miss Jones," she said.

Miss Jones's face went pale with indignation. This was outrageous. It was a bare-faced lie. Why, she'd seen it with her own eyes. . . .

"But I *saw* it there, Mrs. Brown," she persisted.

Really, thought Mrs. Brown, Miss Jones was behaving very oddly. She looked most peculiar and was evidently suffering from optical delusions.

"Come and see for yourself, Miss Jones," she said kindly. "As a matter of fact, we've no Crown Derby in the house."

Miss Jones followed her down the passage to the morning-room and stood there gaping at the mantelpiece. There was the very spot where it had stood, but all that could be seen on the mantelpiece now was the clock and the heterogeneous assortment of oddments that generally stand on morning-room mantelpieces. Miss Jones raised her hand to her head. Was she—was she being *haunted* by her Luck? Was it going to follow her wherever she went, appearing and vanishing, vanishing and appearing? Did it portend some terrible disaster, like stories of white women and people with their heads under their arms in ancient houses? She'd seen it distinctly and now it wasn't there. And Mrs. Brown couldn't have moved it, because she hadn't been out of her sight once during the afternoon.

"I—I must have been mistaken," she said faintly. "It's all very odd. I'm so sorry."

"It's quite all right, my dear," said Mrs. Brown placidly. "I'm always making mistakes myself."

They returned to the drawing-room where Mrs. Monks had finally decided every question connected with the printing of tickets and posters and was now attacking the stalls.

"What's happened to the butter muslin we generally use?" she asked. "I don't seem to have it."

"Oh, no," said Mrs. Brown. "You asked me to keep it, don't you remember? It's in the chest of drawers on the landing. But it really has got a bit bedraggled. I'll fetch it down and show you."

"Let me help you, Mrs. Brown," said Miss Jones.

She felt that she must *do* something or she'd go mad. What could that strange fleeting vision of her Luck have meant? The only thing to do was to get down to ordinary life at once, to carrying and sorting out butter muslin, or—well, *anything* might happen to her.

She followed Mrs. Brown up the staircase, past Ethel's room to the wardrobe. And out of the corner of her eye Miss Jones seemed to see her Luck standing on the mantelpiece of Ethel's room. She daren't look properly, but there it seemed to be—her Luck, plain and unmistakable, standing on the mantelpiece of the bedroom they had just passed. A cold shudder crept through her. Absently she replied to Mrs. Brown's comments on the butter muslin, agreeing that the blue was badly faded, but the yellow wasn't too bad, and they'd all be the better for a good wash. . . .

Then they picked up the bundles to carry them downstairs. Drawing in her breath, and summoning all her courage, Miss Jones stood at the door of Ethel's bedroom and looked in. Yes, there it was—that vision of her

Luck that was haunting her so persistently. She took a step into the room, then terror overcame her and she plunged downstairs after Mrs. Brown, tripping over the length of blue butter muslin in her haste, and nearly falling headlong. In the drawing-room Mrs. Monks presided over a lengthy and voluble inspection of the butter muslin, and again they were all so earnestly occupied that no one heard William return.

For when William was half-way across the fields to Ginger's, a sudden thought struck him. Ethel's mantelpiece was a very narrow one, and she always kept her window wide open, and only last week he remembered her saying that a framed photograph had been blown off it as she opened the door, and the glass broken. That mustn't happen to the vase before he'd collected his threepence. . . . The spare room. Its windows were closed and no one ever went into it. It would be absolutely safe in the spare room till he'd handed it over to Ethel and got his threepence. Ethel, he was quite sure, wouldn't give him a penny if the vase was broken. . . .

He ran home, put his air-gun against the door, hurried upstairs again, took the vase from Ethel's room, put it in the spare room and ran out to collect his air-gun and rejoin Ginger.

Meantime Miss Jones sat trying to calm her fluttering nerves. Why should this mysterious thing be happening to her in this house? What hand had Mrs. Brown in it all? Miss Jones had read a book the other day in which it was stated that magic was still practised and that witchcraft still existed in the most unexpected quarters. At the time she had been impressed but not convinced. Now, however, she wondered. . . . Looking at Mrs. Brown's placid, middle-aged, good-natured face, she found it difficult to believe that she was a witch, but—well, there it was! You couldn't get away from it.

Mrs. Brown was gathering up the butter muslin again. "I'll see to it," she was saying. "There's no need for anyone else to bother. It won't be any trouble at all. I'll put them through the wash tomorrow and give that blue one a dose of Dolly Blue. Then they'll all be ready for the end of the week."

"Let me help you," said Miss Jones, gathering up a few loose ends. She must—she simply *must*—go into that room where she'd seen her Luck and—and confront Mrs. Brown with it. She'd know no peace of mind till she'd done it.

"Thank you so much, dear," said Mrs. Brown, still looking as unlike a witch as it would be possible for anyone in the whole world to look. "That's very kind."

Again Miss Jones followed her hostess upstairs.

"One moment, please, Mrs. Brown," she said, as they reached the door of Ethel's bedroom. "I have something——" She stopped abruptly. Again her Luck had vanished. She sat down on a chair and stared wildly at the spot where the Luck had been. She could hardly believe that this ghastly thing was really happening to her. Haunted. Haunted by a Crown Derby vase.

"You're not well, my dear," said Mrs. Brown kindly. "You've been unlike yourself all afternoon. Now do lie down and rest for a few minutes before you go home. There's quite a comfortable sofa in the morning-room, and you'll be all alone there and no one will disturb you. Come along. . . ."

Miss Jones was past speech. She followed Mrs. Brown in silence to the morning-room and allowed herself to be settled down with a rug. A plan was forming in her mind. Mrs. Monks, she could hear, was beginning to discuss the competitions (she could hear her saying: "Nothing, of course, that would give the slightest opening to horse play in any form'') and that she knew would last about a quarter of an hour. She must act quickly. Her Luck was somewhere in this house and she was going to find it.

As soon as Mrs. Brown had returned to the drawing-room she leapt from the sofa and began to search the room. She opened drawers, peeped into cupboards. . . . No, it wasn't there. She slipped into the dining-room and searched that. It wasn't there. Noiselessly she went upstairs, fearfully she entered Ethel's bedroom—one of the Luck-haunted rooms. No, it hadn't returned to the mantelpiece. It wasn't in any of the drawers or cupboards. She opened the door of the next room and stood tense and motionless. There it was on the mantelpiece. She approached it slowly and cautiously, like a hunter stalking his prey, then pounced upon it suddenly. It didn't vanish this time. It remained solid and tangible in her hands. It was certainly her Luck. She recognised the little chip again and a tiny crack that ran across the base. Oh, this was no ghost, no vision of a vase. It was the vase itself. Someone had brought it here and she was going to find out who it was. Clasping her vase to her breast, her soul flaming with righteous indignation, she walked downstairs and into the drawing-room.

"Not Hitting the Ham, I think," Mrs. Monks was saying, "I've frequently known that lead to horse play." Then they all turned to look at Miss Jones, who had suddenly entered the room, her eyes fixed accusingly on Mrs. Brown, the Crown Derby vase held out dramatically.

"Mrs. Brown," said Miss Jones in an unsteady, quavering voice, "may I ask you to explain how this vase of mine comes to be in your house?"

Mrs. Brown gazed at it, bewildered and concerned.

"But it isn't in my house, Miss Jones. Well, I mean, I

see that it is now, but I've never set eyes on it till this moment."

"Do you deny", said Miss Jones, her voice rising shrilly, "that this vase has been on the mantelpiece of three separate rooms in this house during the last half hour?"

"But of *course* I do, Miss Jones," said Mrs. Brown. "It's an absurd idea. Why *should* it be?"

"Why should it be indeed?" echoed Miss Jones darkly. "That's what I intend to find out. This vase was stolen from my house this morning, and this afternoon I find it in yours. On three different mantelpieces in three different rooms. I intend to have an explanation."

Meantime William, from the window of the attic of Ginger's home (where the Outlaws were trying certain experiments on the water cistern) had seen Ethel returning from her lunch and tea engagement, and hastened out to secure his threepence. He caught her at the gate of his home.

"I've got it, Ethel," he said. "It's on the mantelpiece of the spare room. I thought it'd be nice and safest there. Can I have the threepence?"

She opened her bag and gave him three pennies.

"I hope you've not made a nuisance of yourself to anyone about it," she said sternly.

"Goodness no!" said William, as if amused by the idea. "I should jolly well think not!"

"You've not got into any sort of trouble over it?" asked Ethel apprehensively.

She had felt a little nervous all day at the thought of having let William loose upon the quest. She was relieved to hear that the occasion had passed off without incident. They entered the house together by the side door.

"Oh, bother!" said Ethel, looking at the array of

"IT'S NOT THERE, WILLIAM," SAID ETHEL INDIGNANTLY.

coats on the hat stand. "The Sale of Work people are still here. Where did you say it was?"

"On the mantelpiece in the spare room."

Ethel went upstairs, and William was just slipping out again quietly by the side door when he was arrested by a high-pitched hysterical voice from the drawing-room. Something exciting was going on, and William never liked to miss anything exciting. He went into the drawing-room. Miss Jones was still standing, with her

"NO, IT'S HERE," SAID WILLIAM, POINTING TO THE LUCK.

Luck held out accusingly at Mrs. Brown, and Mrs. Brown, more mystified than ever, was saying: "But, Miss Jones, I've never *seen* it till this minute. It *can't* have been in this house all afternoon. The very idea's absurd. How *could* it have been?"

"You should know that," Miss Jones was saying.

"*You* should know that. All I want is an explanation. All——"

They turned and saw William standing in the doorway.

"William," said Mrs. Brown, "you don't know anything about this vase, do you?"

"Yes," said William. "It's Ethel's."

For a moment Miss Jones was bereft of the power of speech. When it returned to her all she could do was to gasp.

"Well!" She looked wildly from William to Mrs. Brown. She sought for further words, but all she could do was to repeat: "Well!"

"Aunt Lucy sent it her on her birthday," went on William.

"*Oh!*" gasped Miss Jones, nearly dropping her precious Luck in her agitation. "How *dare* you tell such a bare-faced——"

At that point Ethel entered.

"It's not there, William," she said indignantly.

"No, it's here," said William, pointing to the Luck.

"That's not it," said Ethel.

"But you said red and gold," persisted William.

"It was red and gold, but it wasn't that one."

At this point the maid announced Miss Barlow and told Mrs. Brown that she was wanted on the telephone.

Peggy strolled languidly into the room.

"Oh, there you are, William," she said. "I know it isn't important, but I was just passing and thought I might as well tell you that I made a mistake. It's Miss Jones up at Marleigh who has the rummage things, with that vase you wanted to copy, not Miss Jones at Hadley. Hello, Miss Jones! Another vase. Vases, vases, everywhere. Well, I'm really on my way to badminton, so I'll run on. . . . Thought I might just put the budding artist on the right track. Though why it has to be vases, Heaven only knows. It always used to be leaves when I was young. . . ."

Mrs. Brown returned.

"It was my sister to say that she's got 'flu and can't come to us for Christmas. Such a pity. . . . Now, Miss Jones, do explain what you meant about the vase. . . . Ethel, Miss Jones says she saw the vase in your bedroom. It *couldn't* have been, could it?"

"With my own eyes I saw it," put in Miss Jones, on the highest note she'd yet reached.

"Well," said Ethel, "it's a bit complicated, but William said that he'd get the vase Aunt Lucy gave me and he seems to have made a mistake."

They all turned to the spot where William had stood. The spot was empty. Realising that someone had blundered, and strongly suspecting that it was himself, he had sloped off as quickly and quietly as he could to spend his threepence.

Chapter 7

William's Bad Resolution

"I'm sick of this New Year business," said William gloomily. "I don't get anything out of it. Jus' rotten ole good res'lutions an' everyone goin' on at you worse than what they did before."

"I know," said Ginger, "an' they won't even let you have anythin' int'restin' for a good res'lution. Jus' dull things like bein' obedient an' quiet an' clean an' suchlike. Once I tried havin' one to be an adventurer same as you read about in books, but they made such an awful fuss I had to stop."

"Pity *they* don't ever make one to be a bit kinder," put in Douglas bitterly.

The post-Christmas reaction had set in. After the excitement of presents, parties and unlimited food, life seemed to stretch before them—an unending expanse of dullness—and the suggestion of good resolutions made by their parents with tactless references to past misdeeds added insult to injury.

"I can't remember a single good res'lution I've ever made", said William, "that's turned out right. They've all got me into worse rows than if I'd not made 'em. I've a good mind to try a bad one for a change." His look of boredom vanished, and he brightened visibly. "Yes, that's a jolly good idea. I'll have a bad res'lution. It couldn't come off worse than some of my good ones have, anyway."

They looked at him with interest.

"D'you mean bein' disobedient or noisy or dirty or somethin' like that?" said Henry.

"Corks, no!" said William contemptuously. "Nothin' as dull as that! I'll be *reely* bad. Same as people in the newspapers."

"A murderer?" said Ginger awefully.

"N-no," said William. "I don't want to be a murderer 'cause they get hung. I'd be a gambler if I knew how you did it. . . . A man my father knew got put in prison for promotin' a comp'ny, but I don't know how you do that either."

"What *will* you do, then?" asked Ginger.

William considered for a moment.

"Stealin's easy enough," he said at last. "I guess I'll be a burglar."

"What'll you steal?" demanded Henry.

"Well, I can't think of everythin' at once," said William testily. "I've gotter think a bit. I bet all burglars've gotter think a bit. . . . Well, I've gotter find out where things are before I steal 'em, haven't I?"

"Steal somethin' of Hubert Lane's," suggested Ginger. "He's been awful since he heard about his mother's rotten ole heirloom."

Hubert Lane had lately been throwing his weight about even more than usual on the strength of an heirloom that was shortly to come to his mother.

"My great-aunt's bringin' it down," he had explained importantly. "She's givin' all her heirlooms away 'cause she doesn't want to be bothered writin' them down in her will. She's comin' to stay with us at the New Year, an' she'll bring ours down with her. It's a jolly fine heirloom. I bet not many people've got an heirloom like ours."

"What is it?" William had demanded, his curiosity getting the better of his general policy, which was to ignore Hubert Lane except when actual hostilities were in progress.

"We don't know yet," admitted Hubert. "We don't know till she comes down with it. She's givin' diff'rent ones to diff'rent people. It might be anythin' but it'll be somethin' jolly expensive. All heirlooms are jolly expensive. I bet none of you've got an heirloom at all, never mind a jolly expensive one like we're goin' to have."

"We've got hundreds of 'em," William had replied inaccurately, "an', anyway, shut up about it. We're sick of it."

"I say, steal that electric train of his he's always swankin' about," suggested Ginger. "That'll make him forget about his rotten ole heirloom."

William considered this suggestion.

"N-no," he said at last, reluctantly. "I'd like to, but I'm goin' to be a *reel* one. A *reel* burglar. I'm not goin' to steal toys off boys. I'm goin' to steal the sort of thing people steal in newspapers. Jew'l'ry an' suchlike," he ended vaguely.

"Where'll you steal it from?" demanded Ginger.

"I dunno," said William. "I'll have to have a look round first. . . ."

At this point Hubert Lane passed.

"My great-aunt's come," he announced, "an' she's brought that heirloom I told you about. It's a jolly fine one. It's a Whistler."

"A what?" said William.

"A Whistler," replied Hubert Lane. "My goodness! Don't you know what a Whistler is?"

"'Course I do," said William promptly. "I bet I know a jolly sight better than what you do."

"Well, this is a very valu'ble Whistler," said Hubert, swelling with importance till his already plump person seemed perilously near to bursting point. "A very valu'ble one. She's givin' it my mother an' she says she'll have to insure it 'cause thieves'll be sure to be after it. This old great-aunt of mine always sleeps with it on a table by her bed. She says it's worth hundreds an' hundreds of pounds."

"Well, I don't like 'em, anyway," said William firmly. "I never have liked 'em."

Hubert seemed a little taken aback by this.

"Don't you?" he said, then, recovering his poise: "Well, I can jolly well tell you, mos' people like 'em. My great-aunt says she's been offered hundreds of pounds for this one. It's a jolly fine Whistler."

"Oh, go home!" said William impatiently.

"I am goin'," said Hubert simply. "I'm goin' home to tea. I'm havin' jelly."

They watched him out of sight then turned and looked at each other helplessly.

"What are they?" said William at last.

Nobody answered. Even Henry, the omniscient, was at a loss.

"Somethin' to do with whistles, I s'pose," he said—vaguely.

"P'raps it's jus' another word for a whistle," said Ginger.

"It wouldn't cost hundreds of pounds if it was jus' a whistle," objected William.

"It might," said Henry judicially. "It might be made

of gold with jew'ls in, or somethin' like that. . . ."

"It *mus'* be some sort of a music thing," said Ginger, "or it wouldn't be called a whistler. P'raps it's one of those big things they use in bands. I bet they cost a lot of money. The ones with little taps all down them."

"It might be a bird," suggested Douglas. "A sort of whistlin' bird, same as a canary."

"A canary's not worth hundreds of pounds," objected William.

"It might be a special sort," said Douglas. "Some animals cost a jolly lot of money. Elephants do."

"Well, an elephant's not a canary," said William. "There's yards more of it for one thing, an' it doesn't whistle for another."

"But, I tell you, it might be a *special* sort of canary," persisted Douglas. "A pink one or a blue one. I bet a blue canary'd cost a jolly lot of money."

"Anyway," Henry reminded them, "he said she kept it by her bed, so we could easy find out what it was."

"*Tell* you what!" said William. "I'll steal it. I'll have it for my bad res'lution. He said reel thieves were after it, so that makes it all right."

"Yes, but reel burglars steal at night," objected Ginger. "I bet you could never keep awake all night same as they have to. 'Sides, you'd never get in an' out without makin' such a row, you'd wake 'em all up."

"Well," said William, "p'raps I'll start with bein' a daytime one. I s'pect they all start with bein' daytime ones, an' work up to bein' night-time ones gradual. Anyway, it's a reel thing to steal all right, 'cause he said so, an' I can easy see what it is 'cause he said it was on the table by her bed. Bet it's a musical instr'ment."

"Bet it's a bird," said Douglas.

"Might be an anshunt Roman whistle," said Henry.

"You know, whistla. Same as mensa. Ole things cost a lot of money. You've gotter pay pounds an' pounds for a rotten ole Roman penny. I bet that's it. Whistla, whistle. Whistla, O whistle. Whistlam, whistle. Whistl—an' all the rest of it," he ended vaguely.

"Might be somethin' about cards," said Ginger, suddenly propounding a fresh theory. "There's a card game called whist. P'raps it's a machine for playin' it. I bet it's more likely to be that than anythin'."

"We'll know soon, anyway," said William firmly, "'cause I'm goin' to start on it this afternoon."

Directly after lunch he cautiously approached the Lanes' house. It was a pity, he thought, that his personal appearance was so familiar to the household, otherwise he might have gained admittance by pretending to be a gas inspector, or a piano tuner like a real burglar. He toyed with the idea of corking a moustache on to his lips and borrowing Robert's coat, but decided against it on the grounds that he had tried it before and found it an insufficient disguise. No, he must just hang about the house and wait his chance.

The place looked quiet enough. As a matter of fact, Mrs. Lane had asked a few friends to coffee after dinner the night before in honour of her aunt's visit, and both she and her aunt were now in the process of making up their lost hours of sleep, while Hubert was in the kitchen trying to coax the cook to let him finish the apple tart that she had just brought out of the dining-room. So still and peaceful did everything look that William was emboldened to open the gate and walk cautiously up to the front door. He rehearsed suitable excuses should Mrs. Lane suddenly appear and demand an explanation of his visit. "Please, Mother says can you come to tea next Wednesday?" (an awkward situation might arise next Wednesday, of course, but that was far enough off) or—simpler, perhaps, but likely to be more coldly received: "Please can you tell me the time? I've forgot my watch." No Mrs. Lane appeared, however, and he accomplished his journey to the front door in safety. At least, almost to the front door, for just before he reached it he stopped and stood motionless, staring in amazement at the morning-room window. It was no longer the morning-room window. Mrs. Lane's aunt always slept on the ground floor and had refused even to consider occupying the official Lane spare room with it's elegant, peach-coloured curtains and eiderdown, so Mrs. Lane had had to turn the morning-room into a bedroom for her. And there she was—in full view of William—lying on the bed under the peach-coloured eiderdown (which had been brought downstairs for her) fast asleep. William summoned all his courage and approached the french window. The handle turned with a faint creak. He stood there, holding his breath, but the large figure on the bed continued to emit deep rhythmic snores. He looked eagerly round the room. Yes, there was the table by her bed and—yes, it *was* a sort of trumpet. There was only that and a silly sort of picture in a frame, so it must be the trumpet. He'd said so all along, he thought triumphantly. He'd been sure it couldn't be a bird, or a whistle, or a game of cards. He tiptoed heavily to the bed, took up the ear trumpet, slipped it under his coat, made his way to the garden again, closed the window, and fled as quickly as he could to the gate and down the road. When he'd reached a safe distance he stopped and listened. . . . There was no commotion, no hue and cry. He could see the Lanes' house through the trees quite clearly. It lay peaceful and untroubled in the winter sunshine—Mrs. Lane asleep in her bedroom, Great-

Aunt Sarah asleep in the morning-room, Hubert just finishing the last crumb of the apple tart in the kitchen. There was something almost disconcerting about the simplicity of crime.

"Crumbs!" thought William to himself. "I wonder everyone doesn't go in for it. . . ."

WILLIAM TIPTOED HEAVILY TO THE BED.

He carried the ear trumpet to the old barn and proudly displayed it to the Outlaws, who were relieved by his safe return and deeply interested in his booty.

"What sort of a noise does it make?" asked Ginger.

"Dunno," said William. "I've not tried it yet. I was scared of them hearin' an' comin' after me. But it's the whistler all right. It was the only thing on the table by her bed 'cept a rotten ole picture. Bags me first blow. I got it. I'll do it very gentle so's no one'll hear.''

They watched him, tense with eagerness, as he raised it to his lips.

"Don't seem to work," he panted as he lowered it a few moments later, his face purple with effort.

"Bet you don't blow hard enough," said Ginger. "Let me have a try."

He had several tries and finally relinquished it, even more purple-faced than William.

"It's broke," he gasped in a faint whisper.

"Not much of a whistler," commented Henry with heavy sarcasm.

"Bet you don't know how to do it," said Douglas. "Let me have a try."

He had a try. The veins stood out on his forehead, his eyes went bloodshot, his general appearance suggested someone in the last stages of an apoplectic fit, but still no sound came. When he finally surrendered it he was past the power of speech and could only shake his head feebly.

"P'raps you've gotter press a spring or somethin'," suggested Henry.

"No, it's broke," said Ginger. "I bet that ol' Hubert's been meddlin' with it."

"Well, anyway, it's the whistler all right, whether it whistles or not," said William firmly. "Let's try again."

They tried again. They attacked it suddenly as if to take it off its guard. They approached it slowly and gradually as if to coax it to its task . . . they breathed into it . . . they puffed and panted into it . . . and yet no sound came. . . .

"It's tea time now," said William in the faint, far-away whisper that was all that was left of his voice.

"Let's go 'n' have tea an' then come back an' have another try."

*   *   *

William was returning to the barn, refreshed by a plentiful meal, and determined at all costs to make the whistle whistle, when he met Hubert Lane strolling along the village street, looking sulky and aggrieved.

"What's the matter?" asked William, who was anxious to hear if his theft had been discovered.

"My aunt says she's not givin' us that Whistler now," said Hubert. "Mean ole thing!"

"Why?" said William, waiting confidently to hear that the heirloom had been stolen.

"You'd like to know, wouldn't you?" said Hubert disagreeably and walked on.

Actually, when Great-Aunt Sarah had awakened to find her ear trumpet gone, her suspicions had fallen at once upon Hubert. It was the sort of trick boys played on one, and Hubert had been the only boy in the house. In fact the only other people in the house at all had been Mrs. Lane and a staid cook and housemaid—all patently incapable of taking away an old lady's ear trumpet for a joke. Hubert had, therefore, taken it, and unless he gave it back at once, she said, she would go home, Whistler and all. No heirloom of hers should they have, not a penny piece of her money would ever come to them unless that mischievous boy gave her back her ear trumpet at once. In vain Hubert protested and pleaded innocence. Great-Aunt Sarah couldn't hear a word without her ear trumpet and wouldn't have listened to him even if she could. Of course he'd taken it. Well, if he hadn't, who had? It wasn't the first time tricks of that kind had been played on her by boys, and she wasn't going to put up with it.

Hubert, of course, didn't want to tell William this. It showed him in an undignified light, and he didn't like being shown in an undignified light. . . . So he walked on haughtily without further information. William chuckled to himself. 'Course she couldn't give them the whistler. She hadn't got it to give. It was up at the old barn. An' it wasn't much of a whistler either. . . .

When he reached the old barn he found Ginger, Douglas and Henry still forlornly trying to draw a strain from the misnamed instrument.

"Either it's broke," said Ginger, putting the matter in a nutshell, "or we've jus' not got the knack."

"Oh, never mind the ole knack," said William impatiently. "I'm sick of playin' with it. I bet reel burglars don't play with the things they steal. They sell 'em. An' that's what I'm going to do with this ole whistler. I'm goin' to sell it an' get—well, I'm goin' to get a jolly lot of money for it."

"Where're you goin' to sell it?" demanded Henry.

That, of course, was the question. Their minds ran over the village shops—butcher, post office, general dealer—good sound country businesses but not suitable "fences" for a stolen whistler.

"There isn't a music shop in Hadley, either," said Ginger. "There's the toyshop, though. I say, let's try 'n' sell it at the toyshop. It's got mouth organs an' trumpets in."

"No," said William rather irritably. "I tell you, it's a *reel* thing. It's not a toy. It's a grown-up thing an' I'm same as a grown-up burglar. We've gotter——" He stopped, and the gloom of his expression lightened. "*Tell* you what! It's that ole Jumble Sale to-morrow, and my mother's havin' the White Elephant stall. They have reel valu'ble things there. Silver things. I've seen 'em. I'll say can I help her an' I'll put this whistler on the stall an' wait with it till someone comes along an' buys it an' then I'll take the money for it. I bet that's the sort of thing reel burglars do. It's quite fair, too. Well," he amended after a moment's pause, "it's fair in a way. They won't let me have good res'lutions in peace, so I've gotter have a bad one. . . . It's their own fault, but I jolly well wish I'd started on somethin' else than a rotten ole whistler."

Mrs. Brown looked pleased but a little doubtful when William offered his help at the White Elephant stall. She didn't want to discourage the promptings of his better nature, but she had distressing memories of his "help-ing" on former occasions. (Once he had sold the Vicar's wife's coat, which she had laid down on the rummage stall for a moment, for sixpence halfpenny.)

"Well, dear," she said, "it's very kind of you, but, you know, giving change and that kind of thing is a bit difficult. Perhaps," tactfully, "you'll just come and help me arrange the stall and then you can go off and play with your friends. That'll be a great help to me and it won't spoil your afternoon."

But William refused to be put off in this fashion.

"No," he said firmly, "I want to help. I'll jus' stand at the end of the stall an' jus' sell the things there. You needn't worry about change. I can manage change all right. Yes, I know some of 'em made a fuss las' time," he added hastily, "but some of 'em'd make a fuss whatever happened. They *like* makin' a fuss. An', anyway, if their change isn't right they can say so, can't they? They're not dumb, not by a long chalk, most of 'em."

"Very well, dear," agreed Mrs. Brown reluctantly.

"You can help, but you'd better ask people to give you the exact money and come to me if you're in doubt about anything."

"Oh, I'm not likely to be in doubt about anythin'," said William airily.

On the afternoon of the sale he took up his position at the very end of his mother's stall, with the ear trumpet in front of him. Occasionally people asked him the price of other articles, but he ignored them. He'd come there to sell his whistler and that was all he was going to do. He wasn't interested in any of the other white elephants— chipped vases, battered lampshades, stringless tennis racket, rusty gas brackets and the heterogeneous medley that usually haunts such places. Mrs. Brown was pleased to see him standing there so quietly. She'd been afraid that he was going to take a real interest in the proceedings, and when William took a real interest in the proceedings, strange things were apt to happen. The remains of an iron coal scuttle, balanced precariously on a pile of venetian blind slats, hid the ear trumpet from her sight. In any case it fitted in remarkably well with the general atmosphere.

Shortly after the sale had begun Mrs. Lane entered, accompanied by Hubert and Great-Aunt Sarah. Mrs. Lane looked aggrieved, Hubert sulky, and Great-Aunt Sarah grimly determined. She had issued her ultimatum at breakfast. Either the ear trumpet must be restored to her before nightfall or she would return home taking her Whistler with her. In vain had Mrs. Lane protested Hubert's innocence—at first in her loudest voice and then, as Aunt Sarah gave no sign of having heard, on her best deckle-edged notepaper. In vain had Hubert assured her in red crayon on a page torn out of his arithmetic book that he "loved his deer aunty too much ever to play trix on her". Great-Aunt Sarah remained unmoved. No one but Hubert could possibly have taken her ear trumpet and unless it was returned by that evening, no heirloom (or anything else) of hers should ever come to them. . . .

Mrs. Lane had promised early in the week to go to the Jumble Sale, and was quite glad of the diversion. It would relieve her, for a time, at any rate, from the necessity of trying to make Aunt Sarah understand that Hubert could not possibly have stolen her ear trumpet. ("He's incapable, dear Aunt, of an unworthy action," had been her last, but unsuccessful, effort.)

Great-Aunt Sarah entered the Village Hall and looked about her. And at once her piercing eye fell upon the ear trumpet lying on the extreme end of the White Elephant stall. She drew in her breath sharply. So *that* was what the little devil had done—stolen it from her and given it to a White Elephant stall! His idea of a joke, she supposed. She'd *give* him joke! She crossed the room to the stall in order to assure herself beyond a shadow of doubt that it was her ear trumpet. Yes. It *was* her ear trumpet. She'd have known it in a thousand. . . .

"It's a whistler," William was saying hopefully. "It's"—he tried to say "a hundred pounds", but the words failed him, and he ended lamely—"sixpence."

But Great-Aunt Sarah was not listening and would not have heard if she had been. She snatched up the ear trumpet, turned to Hubert, who was standing by gaping at her, and boxed his ears with a vigour surprising in one of her advanced years. Hubert, howling at the top of his voice, fled from the room, and Aunt Sarah turned with a little smile of satisfaction to the interested audience that had gathered round.

SHE TURNED TO HUBERT, AND BOXED HIS EARS WITH SURPRISING
VIGOUR.

"*That'll* learn him," she said. "White Elephant
indeed!"

Mrs. Monks, the Vicar's wife, had come up to the
stall. She hadn't forgotten that little affair of the coat
and had been keeping an eye on William from a distance
ever since the sale began.

"What a strange old lady!" she said. "Quite a charac-

WILLIAM'S BRAIN REELED.

ter, isn't she? Have you seen the lovely Whistler she's brought for Mrs. Lane?"

William's brain was reeling.

"The—what?" he asked faintly.

"The Whistler," said Mrs. Monks. "Don't you know who Whistler was, my dear boy? He was a painter and etcher who lived at the end of the last century. The picture that Mrs. Lane's aunt has brought for her is a most exquisite little nocturne."

William's brain reeled still more as he watched, in helpless amazement, as Great-Aunt Sarah put the end of the trumpet into her ear and entered into conversation with her neighbours. Gosh! No wonder it wouldn't whistle!

Great-Aunt Sarah was feeling highly delighted with herself. She'd got her trumpet back and she'd boxed Hubert's ears. She'd been longing to box Hubert's ears ever since her arrival. . . . Her eyes fell upon William. There was another boy—a nice, honest-looking boy, not the sort of boy who stole people's ear trumpets and gave them to White Elephant stalls for a joke. William, fresh from his mother's hands, looked clean and tidy, and his bewilderment gave him a misleading appearance of melancholy virtue. After the relief of boxing Hubert's ears, she felt generous and expansive. She opened her bag and took out sixpence.

"There's a little New Year's gift for you, my boy," she said.

William brightened. He'd got *something* for it, after all. . . . He decided to put off his burglar career till he knew a bit more about Whistlers and things. Considered dispassionately, his bad resolution didn't seem to have turned out much better than his good ones. But he'd got the sixpence. . . . Though sixpence was less than a hundred pounds, it was better than nothing.

Setting off briskly down the road to join the Outlaws, he decided to do without resolutions at all next year.

Chapter 8

William and the Badminton Racket

William sat on the roof of the tool shed and watched Ethel and her latest admirer, Dr. Horace Ashtead, set off for the badminton club, swinging their rackets gaily as they went.

"Everyone's got one but me," he said bitterly. "Everyone."

A new badminton club had been started in the village and everyone for miles around had joined it. The craze had spread to the younger inhabitants, and the Outlaws had rigged up a net (of sorts) in the old barn. Shuttlecocks, of course, were easily obtained from the senior club, but at first it seemed that the question of rackets would present an insuperable difficulty. Fate, however, was—up to a point—on their side, for Ginger, Douglas and Henry managed to procure discarded rackets from their elders. At first William thought that he, too, could not fail to provide himself with a racket in the same way, but by an unhappy chance the supply of discarded rackets had ceased. He passed from subtle hints to open hints, from open hints to impassioned demands, without success. No one else had any old rackets to give away. . . . Assuming his humblest manner, he approached Ethel and asked her for the loan of hers.

"Only jus' now an' then," he said. "I'd do anythin'

you like for it. Fetch things from upstairs an' suchlike."

Ethel, however, was indignant at the very suggestion.

"I never heard of such a thing," she said. "As if I'd let you even *touch* my racket!"

He was sorry that he'd mentioned the matter to her, as it seemed to arouse her suspicions, and when, knowing that she was safely at the other end of Marleigh, he went to "borrow" it for a little game with the Outlaws, he found the cupboard where she kept it locked, and the key presumably with her in Marleigh. This lack of trust in him grieved and shocked him.

"She's even meaner than I thought she was," he said to the Outlaws when he reported this failure. "Fancy *lockin'* it up!"

He had finally to content himself with a minute racket that belonged to Henry's small sister and that Henry had purloined from her toy cupboard. (So far, fortunately, she hadn't missed it.) It was an undignified, infantile affair barely six inches in diameter, the string sagging and cotton-like in texture—unworthy to be named in the same breath as the others' rackets. They were very kind, however, and insisted on lending him theirs at frequent intervals, but the bitter truth remained that he, the leader, had a paltry toy for his racket, while the others had real, workmanlike weapons. He couldn't help feeling that Ethel was the cause of all the trouble. How easy it would have been for her to let him have the racket whenever she wasn't using it herself! It would, as he pointed out to her over and over again, have actually improved the racket.

"Things *rot*, you know, Ethel," he warned her darkly, "with not bein' used enough. I bet the little you use that racket's not enough to keep it from rottin'. I bet it oughter be used pretty near all the time. I bet it's startin' rottin' now, with you not usin' it enough. I'd only use it when you weren't playin'. . . ."

But it was of no avail. Not only did Ethel refuse even to consider lending him her precious racket, but she continued to keep it under lock and key, and to carry the key about on her person.

Still feeling that, somehow, the solution to the problem lay with Ethel, William turned his full attention to her.

The racket had been given her by Jimmie Moore. There was nothing new about Jimmie Moore. He was just part of the normal Ethel-landscape. Jimmie Moore had admired Ethel ever since anyone could remember, and Ethel always returned to him in the intervals of her more exciting affairs. William considered Jimmie quite the most human of Ethel's young men. He had a sense of humour, and on one or two occasions had helped him out of a tight corner. But there was no doubt that, despite the fact that it was he who had given Ethel the magnificent new badminton racket, he was at present in a state of eclipse. And the cause of the eclipse was Dr. Horace Ashtead, Dr. Bell's new assistant.

Dr. Horace Ashtead was a pale but pompous youth, with a squeaky voice, a slight lisp, and a distressing habit of missing balls at badminton. There was no doubt at all that in looks and general personableness he was miles behind Jimmie, but there was about him a glamorous novelty, and a suggestion of the great world that Jimmie, who had lived all his life within sight of Ethel's home, conspicuously lacked. Dr. Horace Ashtead's father was a Harley Street specialist, and Dr. Horace Ashtead meant himself to be a Harley Street specialist after a few years' general experience. His mother gave dinner parties to important people with titles and went to first nights and Ascot. It was all so very different from the life Ethel knew, the life whose highlights were an occasional garden party in summer and amateur theatricals in winter. She'd never met anyone like that before except in books, and in books she'd never really believed in them. It thrilled her to meet one of these glamorous beings in real life. Sometimes she wished that Horace were as good-looking and amusing as Jimmie, or that he wasn't quite such a rabbit at badminton (Jimmie was the club's star player), but, of course, one couldn't have everything, and there was no doubt at all of Horace's devotion. He proposed to her regularly several times a week, but she always said that she wanted a little more time to make up her mind. He was clever, of course (he seemed so stupid that he must really be very clever), and he had the thrilling background of dinner parties and titles and first nights and Ascot, but it didn't do to be in too much of a hurry about anything. Jimmie tried his best to cut the newcomer out, but even he realised that it was a pretty hopeless proposition. He'd never been to Ascot in his life, and the nearest he'd ever got to a title was second cousin to an honourable, and he'd only met him once. And so Ethel went off twice a week to the badminton club, gaily swinging the racket that had cost Jimmie the vast sum of thirty-two and sixpence, escorted by that future light of Harley Street, Dr. Horace Ashtead.

William studied this situation closely, but couldn't see that it led anywhere, as far as he was concerned. He liked Jimmie Moore and he didn't like Dr. Ashtead, but they were equally useless as sources of badminton rackets. He still had to set off to games in the old barn carrying the contemptible former occupant of Henry's sister's toy cupboard.

And then—as if that wasn't enough—further troubles appeared on his horizon. There took place one of those mysterious re-arrangements of staff with which the surface of school life is troubled at regular intervals, and, instead of the placid, easy-going gentleman who generally taught William French and didn't much care whether he learnt any or not, there appeared a fierce young man with a belligerent moustache, a ferocious scowl and an awe-compelling eye, who, unlike most of the other masters, refused to regard William as his Sedan.

"Seems to think", said William bitterly, "I've got nothin' better to do with my time than his beastly ole exercises."

He most definitely *had* something better to do with his time and he proceeded determinedly to do it, hoping that, as had so often happened before, the new master would, after a fair trial, decide that he was hopeless, and devote his energy to more promising material. But this particular master—Mr. Coggan by name—was pre-eminently of the bulldog breed.

"I can hold out as long as you, my boy," he said grimly, "and before I've finished with you you'll be doing the work you're set and doing it properly."

There came a day when he said that the next time William "forgot" to do his French exercise he would be sent to the headmaster. William, who had had previous and highly unpleasant experience of interviews with the headmaster, decided to bow his head to Fate and for the time being, at any rate, to give his full attention to the French exercises on those bleak and baleful evenings when the wretched things were due.

"It's that or bein' murdered," he said darkly. "The las' time ole Markie had me up he only jus' didn't murder me. I bet he'd do it quite, this time. . . . In a way I'd rather be murdered once an' for all than torchered every week by ole Cogs same as I am now. . . . Anyway, I won't be able to come out to-night. I'll be doin' his ole exercise. I dunno how they think we can live", he continued pathetically, "without any fresh air. People die without fresh air. We had a lesson on it once in Chemistry. An' in Hist'ry. They died in a place called Blackpool somewhere in hist'ry 'cause they hadn't any fresh air. Same as I shall—stayin' in every night, doin' French exercises without oxygen an' suchlike. Fat lot of use French is goin' to be to me when I'm dead. *Or* alive, come to that. Well, I jolly well hope ole Coggs'll be sorry, that's all. . . . Don't suppose he will, though," he ended morosely, as a moment's honest consideration deprived him of even that small ray of comfort.

But he did really intend to devote that evening to his French exercise and he would have done had not a new air-gun, sent unexpectedly by Aunt Louie (who had a pleasant habit of sending what she called "un-birthday presents"), arrived that morning and driven everything else from his mind. He spent the evening hunting happily with it in the woods and did not return home till after bedtime. He went to sleep at once, dreamt ecstatic dreams of putting to flight whole tribes of Red Indians (every one of whom bore a striking likeness to Mr. Coggan), armed only by his air-gun, and did not wake till his mother put her head round the door and said: "You'll never be in time for breakfast, William, if you don't hurry."

Then, and only then, did the full horror of the situation dawn on him.

It was Thursday morning, and he hadn't done his French exercise. Hadn't even begun it. Hadn't written a single word of it. Hadn't even thought of it. And in five minutes' time the breakfast gong would sound and, immediately after breakfast, it would be time to set off to school. His mind leapt nimbly to the only possible solution of the problem. He must be ill. Really ill.

Seriously ill. His mind went quickly over the possible illnesses. Headaches were no good. He'd tried them often. Rheumatism was worse. He was simply laughed at when he tried rheumatism. (That, incidentally, was particularly unfair when he thought of the sympathy that was showered from all sides upon old Mrs. Black when she stayed in bed with it.)

There was lameness, of course, but the last time he'd tried being lame (he had rather a good limp) he'd been taken to school in his father's car and had had, moreover, to try to keep up his limp all day, which was very inconvenient as well as tiring. It was unfortunate, moreover, that his mother, passing the school during the morning recess, should happen to have seen him pursuing one of his foes at breakneck speed round the playground. She showed little sympathy later when she saw him limping slowly and with grimaces expressive of supreme agony up the garden path to the front door.

Headaches, rheumatism, sprains of all kinds were ruled out. Infectious diseases needed symptoms that he had tried in vain to reproduce. He thought rapidly over such of his contemporaries as had recently attained the coveted position of indulged invalids. . . . And suddenly he remembered Johnnie Thorpe. Johnnie Thorpe only put in an occasional appearance at school and was treated by the masters, when he did appear, with a consideration that was accorded to no one else. Johnnie Thorpe had been taken up to a specialist in London, who had diagnosed liver trouble. He bore no such awkward symptoms as rashes or swellings behind the ear. He didn't even limp. He just had liver trouble. There was no time to be lost. Liver trouble, William decided hastily. . . . But where was his liver? On the right, just by his stomach, he thought vaguely. Anyway, he decided desperately, there must be *something* there, even if it

"MOTHER!" HE CALLED IN A THIN, QUAVERING VOICE.

wasn't his liver. . . . And whatever it was must solve the problem for him. . . . He got out of bed and went to the top of the stairs.

"Mother!" he called in a thin, quavering voice. He was rather proud of that voice. It expressed, he fondly hoped, unparalleled suffering heroically endured.

Mrs. Brown came out into the hall and looked up at him.

"My goodness, William!" she said. "Aren't you dressed yet?"

"Mother," said William faintly. "I'm not feeling well."

"Now, William," admonished Mrs. Brown patiently, "don't start that again."

"I don't want to, Mother," said William still more faintly, "but—but I've got an *awful* pain."

He wondered whether to let out a yell of agony at this point, but, being somewhat of an artist and sparing of his effects, he decided to postpone the yell of agony and lead up to it gradually.

Mrs. Brown hesitated a moment then came upstairs. William had got back into bed.

"Now, William," she said briskly, "you know quite well there's nothing the matter with you. Breakfast's ready and you'll only get into trouble if you're late for school."

William let out a low moan (he was still keeping the yell of agony for later).

Mrs. Brown, who was a tender, conscientious mother, looked at him uncertainly. He might, of course, be just up to one of his tricks, but on the other hand he might be really ill.

"Rubbish, William," she rallied him. "If you're *very* quick you'll have time for breakfast and still be in time for school. It's bacon and mushrooms for breakfast. . . ."

She watched him closely. William loved bacon and mushrooms. He left not a scrap or shred or morsel of it on his plate. He offered bribes to Ethel (always without success) for a share of hers. . . . But by a supreme effort of will he contorted his features into an expression of revulsion and did his low moan again.

Mrs. Brown began to feel a little worried. This was different from a limp that alternated between the right and left leg and vanished entirely every few minutes;

different, too, from a rash that had obviously been made with Ethel's lipstick, and a swollen face whose swelling vanished abruptly when he was made to open his mouth. This looked as if it might possibly be serious. . . .

"Where does it hurt, dear?" she asked.

"Here," said William, vaguely indicating a point on the right of his stomach.

Mrs. Brown pressed it tentatively. William thought that the moment had come for the yell and let it out with an effect that startled even himself.

Mrs. Brown's expression of anxiety deepened.

"Just stay in bed, dear," she said. "I'll fetch your father."

William's spirit sank at that, but he decided to stick to his guns and let out a yell whenever that particular spot was touched.

Mr. Brown entered and looked at him suspiciously.

"Well," he said in a markedly unsympathetic tone. "What's the matter with you?"

"He really seems to be in pain, dear," said Mrs. Brown a little reproachfully. "It seems to be here."

She pressed the spot again very gently and William did a groan that was even more effective than the yell.

"I don't suppose there's anything the matter," said Mr. Brown callously, "but you can have the doctor to make sure if you like. . . . I must be off now!"

William was relieved to hear the slamming of the front door that announced his father's departure for the station.

"I'll just get the room to rights before I telephone," said Mrs. Brown, but at that moment there came from the garden the sound of Dr. Horace Ashtead's squeaky voice alternated by Ethel's more dulcet tones. Dr. Horace Ashtead had looked in before beginning his rounds to arrange that he should call for her and take her to the badminton club that evening.

"Five o'clock, then," they heard him say.

Mrs. Brown put her head out of the open window.

"Would you mind coming up here a moment, Dr. Ashtead?" she called. "I'm afraid William's not well."

After a short interval, during which he fetched his bag from his car, Dr. Ashtead and Ethel entered William's bedroom.

"Now, where did you say the pain was?" he squeaked importantly. He was delighted with the opportunity of thus showing off under Ethel's eye.

Mrs. Brown and Ethel stood in the background and watched with respectful interest.

William pointed again to the spot whose choice seemed to be turning out so unexpectedly successful. Dr. Ashtead pressed it so ungently that William's yell surpassed all his previous efforts. Ethel and Mrs. Brown looked at each other with growing anxiety.

"He really *does* seem to be in pain," said Mrs. Brown.

Dr. Ashtead preserved an Olympian calm and proceeded to make much play with his stethoscope as he tested William's heart. Ethel was quite as impressed as he meant her to be. He'd certainly end up in Harley Street at the very least, she thought. . . . He'd probably have a world-wide reputation as the most brilliant doctor of his day. Jimmie Moore faded into complete insignificance by comparison. She couldn't think how she'd ever seriously considered him for a moment. The way Horace slipped those little things into his ears was wonderful. Absolutely wonderful. And he quite obviously could tell exactly what was happening inside William just by those little tappings and pullings about. She'd treat him with more respect in the future than she had done in the past. It was, after all, a wonderful privilege to know a man as brilliant as this. Different from Jimmie Moore and all the other commonplace youths who had, up to now, been her male acquaintances. What did a squeaky voice and a habit of missing the shuttle at badminton matter in comparison with this? The very way he folded up that little telescope thing and put it back into his bag pro-

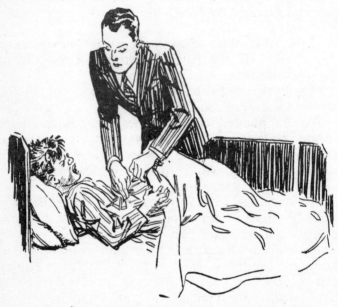

WILLIAM'S YELL SURPASSED ALL HIS PREVIOUS EFFORTS.

claimed heights undreamed of by Jimmie Moore and his like.

"You'll have to stay there for a little, I'm afraid," he said at last and went out followed by Mrs. Brown and Ethel.

William heaved a sigh of relief as the door closed. Well, it had come off all right. He could stay in bed this morning till the French lesson was safely over and then

MRS. BROWN AND ETHEL LOOKED AT EACH OTHER WITH GROWING CONCERN.

stage a recovery as convincing as his illness. The whole thing had been much easier than he'd thought it would be. He was glad he'd had Dr. Ashtead (though he didn't really like him) and not Dr. Bell, who had treated his previous attempts at indisposition with a callous suspicion that had wrecked his most carefully prepared plans. He wished he'd thought of liver before. Liver was evidently child's play. It ought to be good for months and months. Whenever he wanted to escape any particular lesson he could say that it hurt him in that place, and whenever he wanted to get up again he could say that it had stopped hurting. . . . Much easier in every way than limps and rashes and that sort of thing. He lay there congratulating himself upon a discovery besides which the discovery of such things as gravity and America were wholly insignificant and listening to the muted voices of Mrs. Brown, Ethel and Dr. Ashtead on the landing outside.

"It's liver trouble," he imagined Dr. Ashtead saying. "He must just stay in bed till that place stops hurting and then he can get up." With characteristic optimism, he imagined him continuing: "He'd better not go to school for a day or two, but he must go out and get all the fresh air he can."

Actually, Dr. Ashtead was saying, in his squeakiest voice and most important manner: "I'm afwaid it's a case of acute appendicitis. We must get him wemoved to Hadley Nursing Home at once for an immediate opewation."

Mrs. Brown and Ethel stared at him aghast.

"Not an *operation*!" faltered Mrs. Brown.

The Browns all enjoyed the rudest of rude health. None of them had ever had an operation before or even contemplated the remotest possibility of one. The idea that William—William who had been the most riotously healthy of the whole lot—should thus be stricken down, was a terrible one.

"Yes, an opewation," said Dr. Ashtead. "Delay in such cases may be fatal. Fortunately, I think that Dr. Bell is at the nursing home now and he will opewate at once."

Dr. Ashtead was thoroughly enjoying himself. To have Ethel, no longer haughty and capricious, hanging on his words, gazing at him with awe, was intoxicating.

He began to throw his weight about a little.

"I'll send for the ambulance from Hadley if I may use your telephone, Mrs. Bwown. On *no* account, of course, tell the boy himself. He must be kept vewy quiet. . . ."

"There's no real *danger*, is there?" said Ethel anxiously.

"There is always danger in an opewation for appendicitis," said Dr. Ashtead portentously.

He was thinking that, in future, whenever and wherever he and Ethel met, she would see him like this—cool, resourceful, capable, a master of unerring diagnosis, an arbiter of destinies. It should send his stock up tremendously.

While he and Mrs. Brown went down to telephone for the ambulance, Ethel entered William's bedroom.

William looked at her warily. The whispered consultation outside had made him feel nervous. Suppose that, after all, the doctor had seen through the trick and they were planning some diabolical revenge, as they had done when he had simulated a broken leg (that had been the maths master), and they had sent him to school for the maths lesson and kept him in bed the next afternoon, which had been Ginger's birthday party. But Ethel's face did not wear the expression of malicious glee that would have suited such an occasion. Instead, it wore a look of compunction, almost, though William could hardly bring himself to believe this, of tenderness. For Ethel was stricken by remorse. She wished she had been kinder to William. As usually happens in such cases, she forgot the many tricks he'd played on her and remembered only the times she'd been short-tempered and unsympathetic. She decided to do what she could to make up for her unkindness in the time that remained before the ambulance arrived to take him to Hadley.

"It's—it's liver, isn't it?" said William tentatively.

The French lesson would be over by now. He'd wait an hour or so and then start getting better.

"I expect so, dear," said Ethel gently.

William gaped at her, struck speechless by her tone and unusual mode of address. He had just decided that she was being sarcastic and was trying to think of something crushing to say in reply, when she brought out her badminton racket, which she had been holding behind her back.

"I want you to have this, William," she said sweetly.

For a moment William thought that he must really be ill, after all, and suffering from delirium. Things like this didn't happen in real life. Or perhaps he was asleep and dreaming. Perhaps it was all a dream. Perhaps he'd wake up in a few minutes and have to start having liver trouble all over again.

"Th-th-thank you awfully, Ethel," he stammered.

She laid it on the bed and he took hold of the handle. He longed to play with it.

"I'm feelin' a bit better now," he said hopefully.

She looked at him sadly, sighed, said, "Poor William," and went from the room.

William began to feel rather uneasy. It was all so unlike the other occasions when he had manufactured symptoms of disease.

"I say, Mother," he said anxiously, when Mrs. Brown entered the room a few minutes later. "I do feel ever so much better. I can push that place without it hurting now."

But Mrs. Brown wasn't listening to him. She was getting his dressing-gown from behind the door.

"Now, William," she said, "you must be a good boy and do everything you're told."

"I'm ever so much better now," he assured her again.

"I'm sure you are, dear," she said soothingly,

remembering the doctor's injunction to tell him nothing of the impending operation.

"The place doesn't hurt now."

"I'm sure it doesn't, dear," said Mrs. Brown.

"Push it an' see," suggested William.

"I WANT YOU TO HAVE THIS, WILLIAM."

"Not now, dear," said Mrs. Brown.

At first, when William was bundled into a large, waiting car in his dressing-gown, the wild idea occurred to him that they were playing the dastardly trick of taking him to school in this fashion. Then, as the car sped on past the school gates into Hadley, his bewilderment gave way to panic.

"Where are we goin'?" he asked Mrs. Brown, who was sitting by him, gazing at him tenderly.

"Just to see another doctor, dear," she replied.

"I've *seen* a doctor," said William. "It's jus' a bit of liver. I feel *ever* so much better now."

"Yes, dear," soothed Mrs. Brown. "Of course it is. I'm sure you do. . . . Lie back, dear, and don't tire yourself with talking."

"Talkin' doesn't tire me," said William. "That place doesn't hurt any more. I'm all right now, an' I don' want to see another doctor. It's only makin' a lot of expense for you."

"Money is nothing where health is concerned," said Mrs. Brown.

"Yes, but that place is all right now," persisted William. "Push it and see."

"No, it isn't, dear," said Mrs. Brown. "It couldn't possibly have got all right in this short time."

Hearing this, William realised that he must carry on the symptoms for a little longer.

"Well, p'raps it's not *quite* all right," he conceded, "but it will be when I've had a bit of fresh air. Fresh air's all it wants. I don't want to see any more doctors. I've seen Dr. Ashtead an' that's enough."

"Hush, dear. Don't talk so much. You'll exhaust yourself."

A few minutes later William found himself in bed, with his old enemy, Dr. Bell, gazing down at him sardonically.

"Well, where's this pain?" he said. His tone was conspicuously lacking in that tenderness and concern that William had, during the last half-hour, begun to look upon as his right.

"It was a jolly bad pain," said William.

Dr. Bell began to push and pummel him in the region

of his stomach. William didn't like his expression. It was cynical and incredulous. He'd better let out his yell at once or old Dr. Bell wouldn't believe in his pain. He hadn't heard the other yells, of course. He let it out. Dr. Bell happened at that moment to be pressing the left side of his stomach.

"Oh," he said, "so that's where the pain is, is it?"

"Yes," said William. "It's a jolly bad pain."

"I'm sure it is," said Dr. Bell.

He pressed again. William yelled again. He had a vague idea that it wasn't quite the same place as before, but he was so dazed by the swift march of events that he couldn't be quite sure. Anyway, it probably didn't matter to an inch or two. . . . He'd better stick to it now.

"That doesn't hurt, does it?" said Dr. Bell, pressing the right side.

"No," said William.

"But this does?" said Dr. Bell, pressing the left.

William's answer was the finest yell he had yet produced.

Passers-by in the street heard it and turned pale.

But even then Dr. Bell failed to show the concern and sympathy that William expected.

He went abruptly from the room.

Mrs. Brown and Ethel were waiting anxiously outside.

"Are you going to operate at once?" said Mrs. Brown.

"No," said Dr. Bell firmly. "I'm not going to operate at all."

"Oh, dear!" said Mrs. Brown faintly. "Is it as bad as that?"

"I'll tell you how bad it is," said Dr. Bell still more grimly.

"But—perhaps he had stomach ache," said Mrs.

Brown when he'd told her. "He did really *seem* to be in pain."

"I'll put him on a strict diet," said Dr. Bell dryly. "A very strict diet. That should partially meet the case. . . ."

Ethel said nothing. She was watching the glamour slowly fading from the figure of Dr. Horace Ashtead till he became a commonplace youth devoid of charm and good looks and even intelligence. He couldn't play badminton. He couldn't sound his "r's". He couldn't even diagnose appendicitis. He'd never end up in Harley Street and even if he did he'd be just as boring as he was now. She discovered quite suddenly that she hadn't the least desire to have dinner-parties or know titled people or go to Ascot. And the glamour that had faded so completely from Dr. Horace Ashtead attached itself once more to Jimmie Moore. Jimmie, of course, wasn't a doctor, but if he had been she was sure that he'd have known appendicitis when he saw it. Or rather he'd have known it wasn't there when he didn't see it. It would be nice to have an evening on the river with Jimmie again. . . . Every time he'd asked her lately she'd happened to be going out with Horace. She'd tell Horace that she couldn't go to the badminton club with him this evening, and she'd ring up Jimmie and ask him if he'd like to take her on the river. She'd better tell Horace at once.

"Where's Dr. Ashtead?" she asked.

But Dr. Ashtead was no longer in the nursing home. After a short interview with Dr. Bell he had left it as quickly and unobtrusively as possible. He looked as pompous as usual, but just a little pinker. . . .

* * *

William wandered morosely down the lane. He was thinking for the hundredth time that having his appendix really out couldn't be half as bad as what he'd had to endure. He hadn't even escaped the painful interview with the headmaster, for his father had ruthlessly traced the affair to its source, and had sent a note to the headmaster that had resulted in one of the most painful interviews William had ever had. He hadn't even got the badminton racket, for Ethel had taken it out of his room without a word and kept it locked up again in the wardrobe. Moreover, Henry's sister had discovered the loss of the racket from her toy cupboard and had kicked up such a shindy that he'd had to give it her back. William was reduced now to playing with an old coal shovel that he had found in the dustbin.

All things considered he decided that life simply wasn't worth living. . . .

He was passing the Moores' house. Jimmie Moore basked once more in Ethel's favour, and it was rumoured that Dr. Horace Ashtead had applied for a post in a London suburb. He said that there was no scope for a man of his talent in a one-eyed little hole like this.

The story of William's appendicitis had spread, but he still looked so pompous that no one dared to chaff him about it.

Jimmie Moore was coming out of the door with a badminton racket in his hand. William's moroseness deepened. Everyone in the whole world seemed to have one but him. . . .

Jimmie Moore looked cautiously up and down the road, then called: "Hoi!"

William turned and went back to him, scowling ferociously. Jimmie looked at him with a twinkle. He was, he knew, indebted solely to William for his restoration to Ethel's favour. Ethel's favour, of course, was not a very constant quality. It would probably last only till someone more exciting turned up, but meantime Dr.

Horace Ashtead, at any rate, was definitely off the map, and for this, Jimmie, who had disliked Dr. Horace Ashtead intensely, thanked Fate and William. He was making the most of the present. After all, no one more exciting might turn up for months and months. . . .

"I say!" he said to William. "I hear you're in want of a badminton racket. Would you like this?"

William gaped at it.

"B-b-but it's a new one," he gasped.

"Yes," said Jimmie calmly. "I'd heard you wanted one and I happened to be in Hadley this morning and saw this."

"I say! *Thanks!*" gasped William, hardly able to believe his eyes or ears. "Thanks *awfully!*"

Jimmie winked.

"That's all right," he said. "And I shouldn't tell people about it if I were you—not till you're a bit more popular."

"No, I jolly well won't," said William, and added earnestly, "Wasn't it *mean* of her taking it back when she'd *given* it me?"

"I don't know," said Jimmie. "It depends which way you look at it."

"Well, the way I look at it, it was jolly mean," said William firmly.

"I quite see your point of view, of course . . ." said Jimmie.

"I'd better go now or I'll be late for our game," said William, "an' thanks *awfully.* . . ."

He set off down the road at a run. He whistled joyfully. He leapt into the air. He swung his racket exultantly. Despite all its complications, life was, after all, he decided, supremely well worth living.

Chapter 9

William and the Begging Letter

William and the Outlaws sat gloomily in the old barn, brooding on the perennial problem of insolvency. The cricket season was beginning, and all that the Outlaws could muster in the way of equipment was one stump and a handleless bat. They had had, they were sure, a full complement last summer, but everything seemed to have faded away during the winter, as such things are apt to do.

"We had a bat," William was saying indignantly. "I know we had a bat. Can't think what's happened to it."

"We swapped it for a giant Catherine Wheel on Guy Fawkes' day," Ginger reminded him. "Don't you remember?"

"Gosh!" said William bitterly. "Fancy doin' *that*! We must have been batty. Fancy swapping a cricket bat for a rotten ole firework. . . . We had stumps, too. I bet we didn't swap *them* for anythin'."

"No, we used 'em playin' ice hockey," said Ginger, "an' they all got broke."

"Wouldn't you think we'd've had more *sense*?" groaned William, to whom these winter delights now seemed so far away as to belong to another world. "Messin' about with valu'ble things like cricket stumps! . . . What about the ball?"

"Don't you remember?" said Henry. "We set up a coconut shy on the top of General Moult's wall with stones for coconuts and the cricket ball to shy with, an' it went into his cucumber frame an' he kept it."

"He *would*!" said William, and added with still greater bitterness, "S'pose *we* started takin' *their* things off them, a nice fuss they'd make. . . ."

"You can get a set for seven an' six at the shop in the village," said Ginger. "Ball an' bat and everythin'. I saw 'em in the window."

"A fat lot of use that is to us," said William. "We've not got sixpence—much less seven and six."

The finances of the Outlaws happened to be at an—even for them—unusually low ebb. Various domestic misunderstandings had resulted in curtailment of pocket money, and they had recently made a highly indiscreet purchase of a second-hand camera that had turned out to be at least tenth-hand and beyond repair.

Threepence-halfpenny represented the sum total of their resources.

"Threepence-halfpenny!" said William. "An' we're not much likely to get any more either, with all b'longin' to such mean fam'lies."

"I bet we'll be the only ones without 'em," said Ginger morosely. "Hubert Lane's gotter new set. He'll be swankin' all over the place. . . ."

"Funny the way grown-ups seem to get money whenever they want it," said Douglas. "Jus' go to the bank an' get it out. I jolly well wish I was grown up 'cept that they never want to do anythin' int'restin' with their money when they've got it. Why, I knew a grown-up once what paid to learn French. *Paid* to learn *French*! Gosh!"

The Outlaws were silent for a few moments, staggered

by this fresh proof of grown-up imbecility, then William said firmly:

"Well, we've gotter do somethin'."

"Yes, but what?" asked Ginger pertinently.

"How do grown-ups get it?" said Douglas.

"They work for it," said William. "They *say* they work for it, anyway. Doesn't seem much like work to me from what I hear of it. Sittin' about in an office an' ringin' the telephone an' goin' out to lunch with people. . . . I'd like 'em to try *real* work for a bit like what we have to do. I bet I'd sooner ring a telephone and go out to lunch with people same as what they do than have to slave at sums an' French verbs an' stuff till my brain's wore out same as what I have to."

"They don't all work," said Douglas.

"No," agreed William. "Dukes get money left by their fathers an' burglars get it by burglin', but we're not dukes an' I've tried bein' a burglar an' it didn't come off."

"I bet there's other ways," persisted Douglas.

"What are they?" challenged Ginger.

"Well, I dunno . . . but I bet there are."

"I'll try an' find out, anyway," offered William. "I bet there must be other ways, same as Douglas says. All grown-ups can't get it by bein' dukes or burglars or workin'."

Going home for tea, he happened to meet Robert. So engrossed was Robert by his own thoughts that he did not even notice William's presence. He swung along the road, his eyes fixed on vacancy, a fatuous smile on his lips. William looked after him speculatively. There was no mystery, of course, about Robert's financial position. As an undergraduate attending a college whose terms of study seemed to William scandalously short in comparison with those of his own school, he existed precariously on an allowance that seemed to William staggeringly munificent. There was pity as well as envy in William's thoughts whenever they turned to the subject. All that money—and most of it spent on such futile and useless things as socks and ties and cigarettes and even—most pathetic of all—text-books. But William wasn't really interested in Robert at present. Robert, he knew, had made the acquaintance of some people who had come to live at Little Steedham, a village about five miles away, and was pursuing the acquaintanceship with zest. There was, of course, a girl in the case, for Robert was notoriously susceptible, and any fresh arrival in the neighbourhood—if young and personable and of the female sex—was sure, for a time at any rate, to be the only woman whom Robert had ever loved. William had not given much attention to this latest affair. It wouldn't be any different, he thought, from all the others. There was, indeed, a certain monotony about Robert's affairs. They began suddenly, reached their climax suddenly, and as suddenly came to an end, for inevitably, when the charm of novelty had faded, Robert was doomed to realise that the object of his affections was—like the rest of her sex—fickle, irritable, selfish, and not half as pretty as she had looked at first. Idly William wondered whether this fresh affair was worth investigating and decided that it wasn't. What he was after now was money, and Robert, involved in an affair of the heart, was, if possible, meaner than Robert fancy-free.

Dismissing Robert, then, from his mind, William sauntered slowly homeward, his thoughts still occupied by the pressing problem of finance. Where was the money to come from for the cricket set without which the Outlaws' name for the rest of the summer would be mud?

It was Saturday, and William's father was home for

tea. Several other people were having tea there, too, among them a friend of his father's, called Mr. Peters. William slipped into his place and began absently to listen to the conversation.

"Did you see that article in the paper yesterday on begging letters?" Mr. Peters was saying. "Said people made fortunes out of them. Gave several instances—one of a man who kept two gardeners and a Rolls-Royce by posing as a crippled ex-sailor, and another of a man who'd made £3,000 a year by it for years. Had an office of clerks on the job. Quite a business, you know. . . . Curiously enough, I got one myself this morning. I believe I've got it on me. . . ." He took out his pocket book, extracted a letter, and handed it to Mr. Brown. "It would break your heart if you didn't know, wouldn't it? But quite obviously a professional."

Mr. Brown read the letter.

"Yes, almost too harrowing," he commented.

"There is quite an art in it, of course," said Mr. Peters. "Just enough pathos and not too much, you know, and so forth. . . . No, I don't want it back, thanks," as Mr. Brown handed it to him.

Mr. Brown put it carelessly on the writing-table by his chair.

"Like everything else, I suppose, practice makes perfect. Probably sent to the right person that letter would have been good for a quid or two."

"How do they find out whom to write to?" asked Mrs. Brown.

"Club lists," said Mr. Peters, "and lists of donors to charities. Those working on a large scale, I believe, use the telephone directory."

Then the conversation drifted off to other subjects, and soon afterwards the guests took their leave. William had listened enthralled. He'd been right. There *was* another way by which grown-ups made money. Begging letters. Three thousand a year! Gosh! Well, he could hardly expect to make as much as that, but with luck he'd make enough to buy a new cricket set. He went back to the dining-room and, finding the letter still on the writing-table, slipped it into his pocket and took it upstairs to his room. There he read it slowly and carefully. It certainly was a good one. It nearly made him cry. . . .

The next day Mrs. Brown, ever optimistic on this particular subject, remarked to her husband how much better William had been behaving of late.

"He didn't say a word at tea yesterday," she said. "Just sat and listened so quietly and intelligently, and we've not heard a sound from him all afternoon."

William was upstairs in his bedroom, composing his first begging letter.

DEAR SIR,

I am a pore man out of work with eighteen children who are all very ill. My wife is very ill. I am very ill. My mother and father are very ill. If you do not send some money we shall all dye. Besides being out of work and very ill I am def and dum. All my children are def and dum. My wife is def and dum. My mother and father are def and dum. Please send a lot of money to get us all cured. It is very expensive getting cured of being def and dum.

Yours cinserely,
William Brown.

He was pleased with it on the whole, but he had to admit it lacked something the original had contained, some suggestion of suffering bravely even cheerfully endured. In an attempt to convey this he added: "PS. I do not mind being def and dum", then crossed it out, realising that it largely neutralised the force of the appeal. He read it again, frowning critically. No, it wasn't really quite satisfactory. He compared it with the original. It wasn't only what was written. It was the writing itself. The writing of the original was thin,

WILLIAM WAS COMPOSING HIS FIRST BEGGING LETTER.

wavering, indescribably pathetic. William's writing, though highly irregular, was stout and inky and altogether lacked the suggestion of pathos so cleverly conveyed by the other. He'd try copying the original, just altering a bit here and there to make it different. Then a better idea struck him. He'd copy the original as it stood without altering anything. Then an idea struck him so much better than either of these that for a moment it took his breath away. He wouldn't even copy out the original. He'd use it as it was. He'd cut off the top where the address was and the bottom where the writer's signature was, and it would still leave room for his own address and his own signature. His fingers were now covered with ink to the knuckles, but he managed the address and signature without any more blots and finally sat back, his tongue hanging out, his hair standing on end, and surveyed the finished product with satisfaction. It was jolly good. The next thing was to find an address to send it to. "Club lists and lists of donors to charities," Mr. Peters had said, but William had not access to any such lists. "Those who work on a large scale use the telephone directory," he had added. Well, of course, he wasn't exactly working on a large scale yet (though he hoped to be one day), but there was no reason why he shouldn't use the telephone directory. He went cautiously downstairs. No one was about. The telephone directory was kept in the morning-room, where his parents were, but on the hall table was the little note-book where the family jotted down names and telephone numbers. That would do as well. . . . Looking round to make sure no one saw him, William opened the book and turned over the pages. Plenty of names and numbers but very few addresses. The last entry, however, looked promising. It was in Robert's hand-writing. "Lieut.-Col. M. H. Pomeroy, D.S.O., Deep-stone House, Little Steedham." The name suggested ample means with which to satisfy the claims of writers of begging letters, and the address was conveniently distant—a village five miles away, where William was fortunately little known. He went upstairs and carefully addressed the envelope. The necessary stamp took nearly half his available capital, but he hoped to reap a golden harvest from it. . . .

*   *   *

Robert sat at the well-appointed dinner-table and glanced warily at his host. Retired Lieut.-Col. M. H. Pomeroy, D.S.O., was not a man likely to put a nervous guest at his ease. He closely resembled the caricature of the retired military man that so often figures in musical comedy, with the difference that, whereas Robert might have found him funny had the footlights separated them, he found him, at the close quarters of a dinner-table, little short of petrifying. Lieut.-Col. Pomeroy was very large and very red and very impressive in every way. His normal voice was a devastating roar, his most casual glance a ferocious glare. Moreover, the whole atmosphere of the house was, to Robert, as overpowering as the Colonel himself. There was a butler and a footman and a chauffeur—beings whom Robert classed mentally and with awe as "menservants". Robert had been brought up in the simple domestic atmosphere of cook, housemaid and char, with no other male appendage than an occasional plumber and gas inspector. Lieut.-Col. Pomeroy's butler was a kind-hearted man who, in private, could imitate farmyard noises almost as well as a professional, but his public manner was terrific and made Robert feel that he could see right through to his underclothes and knew them to be of inferior quality. When first he met Philippa he had not realised that she belonged to this milieu. She was so simple and frank and jolly and ordinary that he took for granted she belonged, like himself, to the cook-and-housemaid class. They had met at the tennis club and had got to know each other very well. They had been for walks and on the river together. Then she had asked him to dinner, and he found—this.

"Don't be scared of Daddy," she had said. "He's a bit grim, but he's not bad really."

"Grim", Robert now thought, was an understatement. Grim? The man was positively ghastly. . . .

"D'you hunt much?" he barked, fixing Robert with the ferocious glare.

"Er—not much," said Robert, slipping a finger round his collar.

After that he was allowed a few glorious moments of conversation with Philippa. But only a few.

"D'you shoot?" barked his host.

"Er—not much," stammered Robert, whose shooting had so far been confined to O.T.C. practice at school.

Again he was allowed a few moments' respite before the torture began again.

"Did you have many birds last year at your place?" barked the Colonel.

Robert considered. Actually the chief bird inhabitants of the Brown place were sparrows, but he met the eye of the "manservant" who was handing the vegetables, and determined to keep the flag flying.

"Not so many as usual," he said with a fixed and mirthless grin.

"D'you rear pheasants?"

"Not *rear* them," said Robert, implying that he had other and superior methods.

"Partridges?"

Robert's eye grew glassy as he plunged yet deeper into the morass.

"Not a great many . . . not this year."

"H'm. . . . What acreage is your place?"

"Oh . . . pretty small," said Robert.

His throat was dry, he was both hot and cold at the same time, but at least he felt he had carried off the situation with credit.

After that he was allowed to talk to Philippa again in peace. Lieut.-Col. M. H. Pomeroy watched him speculatively. Lieut.-Col. Pomeroy was a man who prided himself on upholding the old traditions. People nowadays behaved anyhow, didn't care what they did or whom they knew, and the Colonel disapproved of it. Philippa, for instance, didn't seem to care what she did or whom she knew. One of the reasons why the Colonel had moved from London was that she seemed to be making so many acquaintances there who failed to conform to the Colonel's standards. Toms, Dicks and Harrys. Rag, tag and bobtail. Young men whom one had never heard of. Young men who didn't seem to know anyone the Colonel knew—or even want to. She seemed to pick them up by the score at cocktail-parties. There weren't any cocktail-parties in the country. There weren't any young men who sold motor cars on commission or hired themselves out as dancing partners. In the country she'd *have* to know the right people. He'd tried to ensure that she did so, and yet even here she seemed to have a knack of getting to know disconnected people out of the blue, as it were. Seemed to pick them out of the hedgerows. People he'd never heard of. People whose people he'd never heard of. . . . This young man she'd brought to dinner to-night, for instance. Looked all right, sounded all right, but you couldn't tell. Not nowadays. He ought to make enquiries. Though experience had taught him that, by the time he'd finished making the enquiries, she'd be well away with the next but one.

"You lived in this neighbourhood long?" he barked suddenly at Robert.

"Er—yes. All my life," said Robert nervously.

"D'you find it difficult to keep a proper staff of servants so far from a town?"

The glassy look returned to Robert's eyes as he stammered:

"Er—no—yes—no. . . ."

"Oh, well," said the Colonel indulgently, "I suppose that sort of thing doesn't worry you. . . . Your parents see to that. . . . Now, butlers, for instance. I find it very difficult to get a really reliable butler nowadays. Don't your parents find that, too?"

Robert turned purple and choked over a mouthful of *soufflé*.

Philippa watched him with affectionate amusement. It was so long since she'd known a shy young man. Her last young man had been world-weary and excessively cynical, and Robert was a refreshing change. His soulful, if slightly codlike eyes following her every movement in goggling adoration appealed to her irresistibly after the sneering grin of the other. His stammering "May I have the honour . . .?" when asking her to dance, was music to ears long accustomed to: "I don't mind shoving you round a couple of times." That in its time had, of course, been music, but variety is the very spice of life. . . .

They had coffee in the library, and Robert opened his soul to Philippa, happily aware that the Colonel was dozing in his armchair. Their conversation dealt chiefly with themselves. Each dwelt at length on the good points of the other and described those startling excellencies that had at first attracted them.

"You're so strong," said Philippa. "So strong and yet so simple."

Robert wasn't quite sure that he appreciated the latter compliment, but hastened to return the ball.

"The minute I saw you," he said, "I said to myself: 'That's the prettiest girl I've ever seen'."

"Did you really?" asked Philippa, whose appetite for this sort of thing was like a monkey's for nuts. "I don't know that I am so very pretty, after all. My eyes", she added, thus drawing attention to her most attractive feature, "are really quite ordinary."

"Ordinary?" echoed Robert, staggered by the girl's modesty. "Why, they're marvellous. Absolutely marvellous. They knock all those film stars' eyes into the middle of next week."

"Do you really think so?" said Philippa. "Some people have told me that I'm rather like Joan Crawford."

"You're twice as pretty," said Robert then, and feeling that even this was inadequate, added: "Three times."

"I think your backhanders are awfully neat," said Philippa, knowing from experience that a few nuts must be thrown occasionally to the nut-thrower, or the interchange languishes.

"Oh, I don't know," said Robert, becoming modest in his turn. "You're marvellous at volleying."

It was at this point that the footman entered with the evening post, and Robert sat up self-consciously and adjusted his tie. The Colonel awoke, said, "Yes, yes, exactly", to prove that he hadn't been asleep, and took the letter from the silver salver. The manservant withdrew. The Colonel looked at the envelope, frowned, grunted, adjusted his monocle, and opened it. Robert and Philippa returned to a contemplation of their mutual charms.

"You do the Lambeth Walk", she said, "better than anyone I've ever done it with."

"Do I really?" said Robert with a gratified smirk. "I don't suppose I could with anyone but you. I'm a rotten dancer usually, but you—bring out the best in one."

Philippa's "Do I really?" died away on her lips, for the Colonel had turned brick red and uttered such a bellow that the very pictures on the wall trembled.

"What *is* the matter, Father?" said Philippa rather peevishly.

She wanted to hear a good deal more about her bringing out the best in people. The world-weary and cynical young man had never discovered that side of her character. She hadn't suspected it herself till now. . . .

The Colonel, whose colour had deepened to a dull purple, was holding out the letter in a hand that shook with rage.

"The audacity!" he shouted. "Lives only five miles from here and has the audacity to send one of his miserable begging letters to me! I know his sort! Read an article in the paper about them the other day. Writes a couple of thousand at a time and gets names and addresses from the directory. Has an office in town. Slipped up over this house, though. Never realised it was so close to him. By Gad, I'll show him up."

Philippa listened with indifference. She was used to the Colonel's explosions. It needed less than nothing to call them forth. The expression of an opinion on anyone's part that differed in the slightest degree from the opinion he happened to hold himself would cause a detonation that could be heard for miles.

She turned to Robert and fixed her blue eyes upon him expertly.

"Do you mean only in dancing I bring out the best of people," she said, "or in other ways, too?"

"Oh, in other ways, too," said Robert, but he spoke nervously, one eye on the Colonel, who was still muttering, "I'll show him up . . . I'll show him up . . ." in a rumbling undertone.

Robert was not used to the Colonel's explosions. He felt that the atmosphere was spoilt for graceful dalliance. Anyway, it was time to go home. He rose.

"Well, if you'll excuse me . . ." he began timidly, for Robert had not quite outgrown youth's agonising uncertainty as to how to take its leave. The Colonel looked at him, realising his presence suddenly after a long interval. Philippa's new young man. Been here to dinner. Bit of a gawk, but, on the whole, an improvement on the last. He must find out more about him, who his people were, etc. Better start now.

"Let me see," he said. "What is the name of your place, now?"

Robert gave his address. The effect of the simple tidings was terrific. The Colonel's face turned almost black. He was, for a moment, speechless, obviously wrestling with some overpowering emotion. When speech did come, though it took the form of three words only, it had the effect of a tornado, an earthquake, a high-explosive bomb.

"You infernal blackguard!"

"Father!" expostulated Philippa.

Robert cringed and quailed with guilt. He had no doubt at all of the meaning of the Colonel's anger. His own conscience, in fact, echoed the Colonel's words. The Colonel, of course, knew the house, knew that its inmates did not hunt or shoot in the accepted meaning of those terms, knew that the only birds its garden normally harboured were sparrows, tits, with, at best, an occasional woodpecker. He had seen through his miserable pretence. He was gloriously and righteously enraged.

"I'm—sorry," muttered Robert, his face crimson with embarrassment. "I—I—I—I didn't realise. . . ."

"I should think you didn't," snorted the Colonel. "I should think you didn't indeed. . . . Out of this house this instant!"

"Father!" expostulated Philippa again and then to Robert, encouragingly: "Stand up to him, Robert."

But Robert was past standing up to anyone. Head bowed, shoulders hunched up, looking like the figure of Guilt in an allegorical group, he followed the direction

"YOU INFERNAL BLACKGUARD!" "FATHER!" EXPOSTULATED
PHILIPPA.

of that pointing finger and did not stop till he found
himself on the road outside the Colonel's estate.

There he stood still, drew a deep breath, and surveyed
the situation. The best solution of the problem seemed
to be instant death, but, despite the emotional stress
under which he laboured, he still felt physically quite
healthy. A pity, because the picture of the Colonel and

Philippa, moved to deep contrition (Philippa by now probably shared her father's anger) by the tidings of his untimely demise, was a consoling one. However, as it seemed out of the question for the present, the next best thing was to remove as far away as possible from the scene of his humiliation. He made tentative proposals to this effect later in the evening.

"I should have thought you'd have wanted a change from this place, Father," he remarked casually, when Mr. Brown had settled down with his pipe and evening paper.

"What do you mean, a change from this place?" said Mr. Brown, in a voice that did not encourage further discussion of the theme.

"I should have thought you'd have wanted to—to—well, to live somewhere else," said Robert, "to—well, just have a sort of change of scene. I think it's—good for people to have a change of scene. We've lived here ever since I can remember. You know, get to know fresh people. One gets tired, I think, of knowing the same people year after year."

"If you've got yourself into any sort of trouble, my boy," said Mr. Brown, taking his thoughts for a moment from the financial page, "you'd better tell me straight out without all this beating about the bush."

"Of course I haven't," said Robert hastily. "Nothing of the sort. . . ."

"Then stop talking through your hat," said Mr. Brown, returning to the financial page.

Robert went out of the room. It was extraordinary, he thought bitterly, how everyone in the whole world seemed to despise him. . . . William was in the hall in his dressing-gown, having obviously just slipped downstairs.

"What are you doing here?" snapped Robert, glad of

an excuse to vent his irritation on someone.

"I'm jus' seein' if I've gotter letter," said William, examining the letter-box. "I'm expectin' a letter, a jolly important letter."

"You!" sneered Robert, working off some of the load of resentment with which his spirit was burdened. "Who d'you think's going to write to you? No one out of a lunatic asylum'd be so batty."

"All right," said William, mentally crossing Robert off the list of those who would benefit by his generosity when he was a wealthy and established writer of begging letters. "All right. I 'spect it'll come to-morrow anyway. An' you'd be jolly surprised if you knew about it," he added mysteriously.

"Yes, I would, wouldn't I?" said Robert sarcastically, little dreaming how surprised he would actually be in that case.

The next afternoon Robert had arranged to play in a tournament at the tennis club, and his first instinct, on waking from a night during which the Colonel, in various horrible disguises, had pursued him relentlessly from dream to dream, was to ring up the secretary and tell him that he had sprained a muscle and would be unable to play. Philippa would be there, of course, and nothing in the whole world, he thought, would induce him to meet Philippa face to face again. He saw the rest of his life as one long, unending series of manœuvres to avoid meeting Philippa face to face. He wished his father had been a little more sympathetic about his plan for removing the whole family to some remote spot. After a large break-fast of poached eggs and sausages, however, something of his courage returned to him. He didn't want to miss the tournament, and even if Philippa were there, he needn't speak to her (not that he need worry about that, he told himself bitterly. After last night she wasn't likely to give him a chance to speak to her). If he saw her at one end of the room, he could stay at the other and so on. And even if he had to play with her, they needn't take any notice of each other. After all, he couldn't spend the rest of his life inventing sprained muscles in order to avoid meeting her. . . . He'd better take the plunge.

He found William hanging about the hall again after breakfast.

"Still expecting a letter?" he said with kindly amusement.

"Yes," said William grimly, "an' it's pretty sure to come to-day, too. I bet you anythin' it'll come to-day."

The tennis tournament turned out unexpectedly well. He managed to avoid Philippa and, considering the nervous strain under which he laboured, played not too badly. At the end he waited till about five minutes after Philippa's departure before he set off homewards. It was with mingled dismay and exultation that he found her outside in her small green sports car, obviously waiting to give him a lift as usual. He blushed furiously, hesitated, then obeyed the invitation of the door she swung open to receive him. They drove in silence for some moments. Philippa had not the slightest doubt that Robert—or, at any rate, his father—made a handsome profit out of begging letters. He was, in fact, a criminal. She was thrilled and exhilarated by the knowledge. She'd never known a criminal before. The situation held all the charm of novelty, with a glorious dash of adventure. She had made up her mind to reform him. . . . Hadn't Robert himself said that she brought out the best in people? He'd been referring, of course, to the Lambeth Walk, but had made it quite clear that the remark had a wider application.

"Robert," she said, narrowly avoiding a lorry at a

bend in the road (her driving was of the hit-or-miss school), "how *could* you?"

Again shame overwhelmed Robert.

"I—I'm terribly sorry," he stammered.

"I suppose you forgot that our house was only five miles away."

"Yes . . ." agreed Robert.

He couldn't help feeling that she was making rather too much of a song and dance about it. After all, he'd never actually *said* he shot or hunted or reared pheasants. But he had realised from the first that she was an exceptionally noble and high-minded girl. . . .

Again she drove in silence for some moments, during which an oncoming cyclist took refuge in the ditch for safety. Then she said:

"Where's your father's office?"

Robert told her, glad of the change of subject.

"You don't work with him yet, do you?" said Philippa earnestly.

"Not yet," said Robert. "I shall go there when I leave college."

"Don't, Robert," Philippa implored him earnestly. "*Don't!*"

Robert's head fairly spun at this, but he was familiar with the situation, so common in books and plays, of the gifted artistic son's being forced against his will to enter his father's office. Though it didn't accord with facts in his case, he realised that it was romantic, and he didn't want to dispel any possible romance that might still linger about him after the unfortunate episode of last night.

"Well . . ." he compromised, "I don't know that there's anything else I could do."

"*Surely* there is!" she urged.

He couldn't bear to quell this flattering interest.

"I—I did once write a poem," he admitted un-certainly.

"That would do," she said. "Anything would do rather than——"

"I don't think I could earn any money at it," he objected, "and my father's business brings in quite a decent income."

Philippa shuddered.

"But it's so *ignoble*," she said.

"Well, I don't know . . ." said Robert, the worm in him beginning to turn at this. After all, though they couldn't keep menservants and didn't run to anything much in the way of birds beyond sparrows, "ignoble" was a bit thick. "I don't know . . ." he said again.

But they had reached the lane that led to Robert's house now, and she stopped the car to let him get out.

"Whatever happens, Robert," she said mysteriously as she took her leave of him, "you'll find that I'm your friend."

Robert stood open-mouthed and watched her drive away. Looking back over the conversation, it seemed to him the oddest he had ever taken part in. . . .

Philippa drove recklessly homeward, pursued by the curses of a cyclist, two pedestrians, and a Buff Orping-ton, all of which she had narrowly missed running down. For Philippa was in the grip of an idea. The details still needed working out, but as an idea it was perfect. From the beginning she disliked her father's plan of simply handing the case over to the police. It was crude and obvious and lacked the human touch. There was a strong streak of romance in Philippa, which even the world-weary and cynical young man had failed to kill. She liked romantic books and romantic films. She didn't care how improbable they were as long as they were romantic enough. . . . And she'd read a book last night that had impressed her very deeply.

A detective had got on the track of a band of criminals. The chief of the band had put an advertisement in a
daily paper in code telling his men to assemble at a
certain time and place, and the detective, who had
discovered the code, had sent an answer, "I'll be
there", and signed it by his own name, which they all
knew. It was a daring and cunning move. It showed them
that he was on their track. It forced them to alter their
plans. It was a sort of challenge. That it threw away his
advantage didn't matter, because he was the kind of
detective who won hands down at every turn. Philippa's
idea was that she should do something like that to
Robert's father, who was evidently the chief of the
begging-letter-writing concern, something to warn him
that she knew all, something to make him change his
plans. . . . It would, at any rate, hold the affair up till
she'd had a chance of reforming Robert. It was obvious
from their conversation to-day that he wasn't yet wholly
given up to a life of crime. . . . But it was rather difficult
to adjust the details. There wasn't any code, for
instance. . . . And then, quite suddenly, the whole thing
became clear to her. She'd writing a begging letter to
Mr. Brown that should be a palpable imitation of his
own and sign it with her father's name. He wasn't
exactly a Scotland Yard detective, but he was a well-
known upholder of law and order. His very name would
strike terror into evil-doers. It would show Mr. Brown
that a man who had held a high position at the War
Office, and who had been a J.P. in three counties, was on
his track.

Her father fortunately was out when she got home,
and she found Mr. Brown's letter on the table. She
copied it—altering only the disability from which the
writer was supposed to be suffering—signed it by her

father's name and despatched it to Mr. Brown's office.

*   *   *

"Are you *sure* there wasn't a letter for me?" William asked his mother despondently.

"Of *course* there wasn't, dear," said his mother patiently. "I keep telling you there wasn't. Whoever do you expect to write to you? It isn't your birthday or anything."

"You wouldn't think anyone'd be too mean to give a bit of money to a pore ole man with no legs an' nothin' to eat, would you?" he went on bitterly.

"No, dear," said Mrs. Brown, "but what's that got to do with you?"

"Nothin'," said William hastily, realising that the less said about that the better. "Nothin'. I was only thinkin' it was jolly mean, that's all. For all *he* cares the pore ole man's starved to death by now."

"For all who cares?" demanded the mystified Mrs. Brown. "What old man? What *are* you talking about, William?"

"Nothin'," said William. "I was only thinkin' that people are jolly mean, that's all. I bet if I had a lot of money an' I heard of this pore man with no legs starvin' to death, I'd send him a shillin' or two. Well, acshully, I'd send him seven an' six."

But Mrs. Brown had other things to do than puzzle over William's cryptic utterances.

"I'm sure you would, dear," she said absently. "Now, don't leave those marbles on the floor. Your father will be coming home soon, and you know he doesn't like seeing your things all over the place."

"Mother," said William slowly, pocketing the marbles, "if you knew of a pore man without any legs starvin' to death you'd give him some money, wouldn't you?"

"Of course, dear," said Mrs. Brown and, looking at him critically, added: "How quickly your hair does seem to grow! I'd better take you into Hadley and get it cut to-morrow."

"Mother," said William, "if you'll give me the money for the pore man, I—I'll give it him."

"Don't talk such nonsense, dear," said Mrs. Brown mildly. "If there were such a man he'd be in some sort of an institution. You let your imagination run away with you. . . . It's hardly any time at all since you had it cut last. It would look better if you remembered to brush it now and then."

"Will you give me the money you'd give the man for cuttin' it," said William, without much hope, "an' I'll cut it myself? I bet I could do it as well as what he does. It'll save you money 'cause you won't have the 'bus fares to Hadley."

"Now, William, don't be silly," said Mrs. Brown. "Of course I shan't do anything of the sort."

William sighed. The begging letter had obviously met with no response. He decided to try the forlorn hope of a direct appeal.

"Will you give me seven an' six for a new cricket set, Mother?" he asked. "I've not got one an' I'll probably get ill with not havin' enough exercise if I don't have one."

"No, William, I won't," said Mrs. Brown firmly. "You know your father said you were to have no more money till that bathroom window had been paid for."

For William had been playing "golf" on the lawn with a walking stick and a potato the week before, and an unfortunate error of judgment had sent the potato through the bathroom window.

"Bathroom window!" echoed William, with a bitter laugh. It was such a good bitter laugh that he decided to make his exit on it. Evidently there was nothing to be got out of his mother in any case. . . . He decided to go to his bedroom for the remaining twopence of his capital, reluctantly report the failure of his attempt to the other Outlaws, and suggest that they spend the twopence on toffee-apples. It wasn't much use saving it, as they weren't likely to get the remaining seven and fourpence, as far as he could see, and he needed a toffee-apple to cheer him up after all this trouble for nothing. Or sherbet. No, toffee-apples were more comforting. He looked in the letter-box on his way through the hall, but it was, as he expected, empty. . . . He repeated the bitter laugh and went upstairs. . . .

* * *

"Oh, by the way," said Mr. Brown to his wife. "You remember what old Peters was telling us the other day about begging letters."

"Yes," said Mrs. Brown, looking up from her knitting.

"Well, it's rather odd," went on her husband, taking a letter from his pocket book. "I had one sent to the office this morning. From an address at Little Steedham. Only five miles from here."

"How extraordinary!" said Mrs. Brown. "What name?"

"Pomeroy."

Mrs. Brown was so surprised that she dropped two stitches.

"But those are the people Robert's just got to know there. He says that they have a big estate and live in tremendous style."

"That's what Peters said, isn't it?" said Mr. Brown.

"Probably got my name from a list with hundreds of others and never noticed that it was only five miles away. What sort of a man is he?"

"I think Robert said he was rather an overpowering sort of man. Very big. Shoots a lot and that sort of thing."

"According to the letter," said Mr. Brown, "he is suffering from a horrible complication of diseases that have deprived him of the power of speech and movement. He has an aged mother entirely dependent upon him, and it is several months since either of them have tasted anything but potatoes."

"Why, Robert said that they have four-course dinners every night. And generally some sort of game."

"He evidently makes quite a good thing out of it," said Mr. Brown.

"Are you going to do anything about it, dear?" said Mrs. Brown.

"I don't think so," said her husband easily. "He'll probably make trouble enough for himself soon enough without my bothering to make it for him."

It was at this moment that a series of resounding knocks echoed through the house, and Lieut.-Col. Pomeroy himself entered the room close on the heels of a flustered housemaid. He had been infuriated by the refusal of the local police to take seriously his accusation that Mr. Brown was a professional writer of begging letters. It was obvious, of course, that either the fellow had bribed them or that he'd covered his tracks so cleverly that it needed a master-mind to bring him to justice. Lieut.-Col. Pomeroy considered himself that master-mind, and he had determined to confront the fellow with his wretched letter and extort a confession from him. Philippa was in the car outside. She didn't know how matters were going to turn out, but thought she'd better be on the spot to keep an eye on them.

Lieut.-Col. Pomeroy stood on the threshold, purple-faced, breathing heavily and glaring at Mr. Brown.

"By Gad, sir!" he spluttered. "You move about extremely well for a man with no legs."

Mr. Brown stared in amazement at this extraordinary opening.

"And those clothes you are wearing", continued the visitor, "would hardly come under the heading of 'rags', one would think. . . ."

"I beg your pardon," said Mr. Brown quietly, "I don't think I caught your name."

"Pomeroy," bellowed the visitor. "Lieut.-Col. Pomeroy of Little Steedham."

"Ah!" said Mr. Brown, taking the letter from his pocket. "Then may I congratulate you on the sudden restoration of your faculties? Your health, I take it, has not been seriously impaired by your recent diet."

He handed the letter to the Colonel, who had taken his own letter from his pocket. In silence each read the begging letter the other had received. In silence each recognised his offspring's handwriting. Simultaneously the Colonel ejaculated, "Philippa, by Gad!" and Mr. Brown: "Good Lord! William!"

Philippa was brought in from the car. William was brought down from his bedroom.

Philippa's explanation was somewhat involved. "I wanted him to know that I knew," she said earnestly. "I wanted to save Robert. I thought he was worthy of better things."

William's was simpler. "I wanted a new cricket set."

At this the Colonel's air of rage and bewilderment left him. The situation had suddenly become clear. He flung back his head and roared with laughter. He slapped his thigh and roared again. Every ornament in the room jingled.

"That's good!" he said when he had recovered his power of speech. "By Gad, that's good! I shan't forget

PHILIPPA'S EXPLANATION WAS SOMEWHAT INVOLVED.

that in a hurry. Wanted a new cricket set!" His laughter bellowed forth again. "The little devil!" He put his hand in his pocket, drew forth a handful of silver, and picked out three half-crowns. "There you are!" he said, handing them to William. "That's towards your artifical